DISCOVER TROLLS, WITCHES AND MAGIC IN
MAXIM'S ALL NIGHT DINER.

WHERE EVERYONE WHO IS ANYONE IN THE
WORLD OF MAGIC GOES.

MAXIM'S ALL NIGHT DINER

Mikka Haugaard

Published in the UK by Everything with Words Limited
3rd Floor, Premier House,
12-13 Hatton Garden, London EC1N 8AN
www.everythingwithwords.com

Printed and bound in Great Britain by Clays Ltd, St Ives plc

A CIP catalogue record for this book is available from the British
Library.

ISBN 978-1-911427-00-1

A brief history of trolls and witches

You are about to read a book about witches and trolls. What do you know about witches? When did you last see one? Do you often talk to witches or are you one of those human beings who can't even recognize a witch when she's sitting right next to you on the train, putting on her make-up in that careful, surreptitious way witches have of doing things when they can feel that you're looking at them? They can spin shadows to cover their faces like masks when they don't want to be seen. Perhaps you prefer trolls. Trolls are hairy and have tails. Of course, some hide their tails and humans can be terribly hairy too. No, it's not always easy to recognize a troll, even if it is easier to recognize a troll than a witch.

The world is full of us. We've been around for a long time, even longer than you. Going back deep into time, you'll discover that this has always been a troll infested planet, and it's better left that way in my opinion—but then I'm a troll. Most scientists agree that humans and trolls diverged from a common ancestor between six and eight million years ago. We kept our hair, our tails, a feel for magic and our awesome strength. Witches and humans are much more closely related— the genetic difference between them is so small that it can difficult to tell them apart, even for someone like me who spends so much time with witches. I've sometimes mistaken a human being for a witch, but I don't mind. Human beings can be good company too, though most of them are not as good story tellers as witches. They don't make you laugh as much, but they are less creepy. Less dangerous. And their familiars are often friendlier and less likely to spy on you, but they're generally clueless when it comes to potions or magic.

We trolls tend to be solitary creatures. We come from the cold north, the mountains of Norway and the frost bitten planes of Siberia, living in caves, on mountain peaks, or in deep dark woods that stretch so far they seem endless. I'm an unusual troll because I quite like company. There's a famous poem composed by a troll which is quoted in a book called the Edda, written eight hundred years ago.

I am a troll,
Friend of the moon
And she who knows the future
Stealer of giants' gold
And swallower of the sun!

That's the sort of big-headed things that only a troll would go around saying and that's probably why some people believe that trolls are not nearly as clever as witches.

But that don't be mislead: trolls can be ever so cunning, but they like to talk big. You have to watch out for any creature who knows magic. You have been warned—but now you must start reading the book about my Diner, where trolls, goblins and witches meet.

Maxim, the troll

CONTENTS

For all those who love scary stories

1

The House of Magic

HE LOOKED ABOUT nine. Quite tall, his hair a deep green, a great lick of it falling across his face.

'I like your hair,' I said.

He didn't answer. He just stood there, looking at me, as if we knew each other. I was busy taking notes for my book about witches and magic. I have been writing it for a long time and I take my notebook with me wherever I go. It's a special notebook with a black velvet cover and some weird gold characters that look Chinese. It comes from a shop on my street where you can buy the strangest things. The woman who runs the shop, all rings, tattoos and a loud voice, gave it to me. Someone had written my name in it. Annabel, it said in beautiful writing and that felt like good luck, although I couldn't think who might have left it. The notebook fits neatly into a small bag I have. You never know when you will discover something new about magic or witches that needs writing down.

I live in London and there are quite a few witches there, though not as many as you would expect. Not when you think how big London is and how old. Witches like places that are big, so they can hide, and they like anything old because it reminds them of the time when there was more magic about than there is now. Far more, though it's surprising how much magic you'll find, if you look in the right places and read the right books. You are reading one now. So if *you* are interested in magic, you are doing the right thing.

I was sitting on the top deck of a red London bus. I always sit there because you get a better view, and I like to see everything. I was holding a pen in my hand because I was taking notes about witches. I was talking to myself because travelling on buses for a long time can make you behave in all sorts of funny ways. Particularly if you live in London. Believe me, it's a crazy place, one of the craziest places on the planet.

'I want to know *everything*,' I was saying to myself. '*Everything* there is to know about witches.'

I didn't expect anyone to answer. I was just whispering very quietly to myself, so quietly that you would need a very special ear to catch any sound at all.

'I want to know about witches and magic, and I want to know everything. Everything there is to know.'

The boy with the green hair was still standing next to me and I could tell that he was listening. I'm not used to people listening to me, but he was listening alright, breathing in that quiet way people do when they want to hear every word and don't want to miss anything. He had a soft voice.

'If you want to know about witches,' he said in a whisper so soft that I half expected to find no one there, 'then I will tell you. But only if you want to know *everything*. Think about it. Because you might not *want* to know *everything*. But with me it's everything or nothing. And what you know,' he added thoughtfully, 'you can't *unknow*. So you better be sure.'

Now I had to look up. I had to see his face. He had blue eyes, a few freckles, glasses and, of course, that green hair.

'I'm Patrick.' He smiled and nodded. 'I'm getting off here.'

So was I. It was my stop, just opposite some lost London plane tree that must have rooted itself there by mistake among the grey houses. I followed him. He went down a street I know well because it's just next to the one where I live, but I didn't recognize it at all. It had grown longer and the houses weren't how I remembered them. The further I walked, the stranger they became and there seemed no end to that street. It slung itself from the main road like a reptile, twisting and turning. On either side there were trees, and gardens. Some big, some tiny, but all of them overgrown with strange plants, I had never seen. There were no people, except the boy I was following. He was walking along quickly and I almost had to run. Finally, he stopped in front of the last house in the street. He looked back and nodded at me. From his pocket he took out a huge rusty key which he fitted into a large, dark wooden door. Carefully, he opened it. I could see a long empty hall.

'Come,' he said.

I followed him wondering whether I should be there. The place had an eerie sense of solitude. I stopped and he turned round and looked at me. There was nothing special about him, except that his hair was green, a very dark and shiny green, as if he were wearing a pile of leaves on his head. He was looking at me in the way he had on the bus, as if we were special friends and the rest of the world didn't matter.

'I've come,' I said slowly. 'I have come to find out about witches. You said you would tell me about witches.'

'I said I could tell you *everything* about witches,' he corrected me gently. 'Do you want to know that?'

'Course I do,' I said, but I wasn't so sure. I thought I could already feel them there, those witches. Breathing the same air as me, their huge eyes on my face, their thoughts big and awesome in those ancient heads on thin, wrinkled necks.

'Everything about witches. Are you ready for that?'

I nodded

'Then follow me.' He turned and began to walk more quickly and I knew that I couldn't turn back.

It was an old, damp house. In every room water was dripping from the ceiling. Along the walls, moss was stretching green spider fingers saying, 'that's mine.' Everywhere there was junk piled high. We went from one room to another. Sometimes we had to climb over dead and broken furniture. Finally, we sat down on an old black sofa, all covered in silver moons and stars.

'Please tell me about witches,' I whispered.

'Do you really want to know?'

'Yes.'

'Last chance. It's your last chance. Do you *want* to know?'

With one finger I drew a yes across a couple of stars. He smiled and turned towards me but I could tell that his thoughts were somewhere else. He was so serious.

'It all happened a long time ago when I was little, but I'll tell you, if you don't mind the risk.'

'The risk?'

'There is a danger.'

He went quiet and thoughtful. I didn't like the silence of that ghost house with its ghost furniture, and that feeling of something I couldn't see somehow being there.

'What danger, what risk?' I asked.

'Well, it's like this: what you know, you can't *unknow*.

Remember that. And there are still witches around, do you want to meet them? Are you ready?'

'Yes,' I replied, but I wasn't sure.

'It's a long story and it begins in an ordinary sort of way. Most stories about witches do. But once you start listening you can't stop. You know that, don't you?'

I nodded.

'And then, of course, there is a *risk*.'

I looked at him very quietly to make him realise that I understood, and that I was prepared.

'There is a risk, because everything is still happening. The story doesn't end although it's got a beginning. All stories begin somewhere, but they don't all end anywhere. So you will have to agree.'

'Agree to what?'

'Agree to become part of the story.'

He rubbed his eyes and looked at me and I could tell that he knew that I would agree, just as water has to go down a plug-hole once the plug is gone. It has no choice. I nodded but I didn't say anything. I just nodded silently listening to the drip, drip of water. There were even plants growing out of the floor. It was as if no one had lived there for a really long time, hundreds of years perhaps. Not real people anyhow. Ghosts perhaps. Or witches.

Then I noticed that someone else was listening as well as me. He was sitting on an old trunk by a window. A tree had shoved one of its branches through the broken glass. The leaves were covering part of his face, but most of it I could see: a big nose, wide lips and bushy eyebrows. He was very pale except for his dark eyes and hair. His clothes were the sort pirates wear, the kind you read about in books: big baggy trousers tied into place with a red piece of cloth, huge boots and a funny hat. Catching my eye, he smiled and put a finger to his lips. I couldn't take my eyes off his hat which looked like a ship turned upside down with the masts and rigging hanging down, making an awesome frame for his face.

'Do you like my hat?' he asked. 'If you do, just look round. This is a glorious place for anyone who likes hats. There's pure genius in the hats. Pure genius—no magic. No magic at all. The magic and the witchcraft are in everything else. The hats, on the other hand, are the real McCoy. Just feel mine: quality felt, silk and silver. You can come over and touch it if you want, but I won't let anyone else wear it.'

I stood up and began walking over to feel his hat, and, as I did, I noticed that there were hats everywhere—which I swear hadn't been there before. Hats with feathers, hats covered in fur. They lay there, as if they had grown out of the ground, like mushrooms in that damp room. Hats shaped like churches, hats that looked like towers, hats like ships, even strange animals.

'Don't come any closer,' he said. 'Or you will be

stepping on hats.' Again he put a finger to his lips to stop me speaking. He rose from where he sat and left the room like a shadow.

'He always leaves suddenly,' said Patrick. 'But you'll meet him again. I'm glad he's proud of his hat, because I know the guy who's made it and he's a glorious maker of hats. Makes them for witches too, and they're difficult customers.'

'Who was he?' I asked.

'He's called Sinbad. He's a sailor who has been all over the world, sailing the seven seas. He tells some crazy tales. Some I think might be true, but others are just awesome lies. You'll see him again and when you do, you'll probably need him, as I once did, or the Queen of Witches would have turned me into a ding dong dangling skeli, skeli skeli thing and I wouldn't be sitting here now, but be dangling in the wind, in the way of her skeli things...'

'Skeli what?'

'Skeli, skeli skeletons. She hangs them in her garden where they ding dong dangle in the wind. Why she does that no one knows, but we'll come to that later.'

'Tell me now.'

'About the Queen of Witches?'

'Yes.'

'You are sure, quite sure?'

I smiled. There was no turning back now.

'You'll get to know all sorts of things, some of them awesome.'

I nodded.

'And what you know, you can't forget—not where witches are concerned.'

He lapsed into silence. I though he might have forgotten I was there. Then he put his hand on my lap and continued slowly, looking at me as if he wasn't sure I should have come.

'You understand that there is a *risk...there is danger.*'

'I do.'

'Then I'll tell you everything I know about witches and magic. It started a long time ago, Annabel, but it's still going on. Still continuing and it always will be, if you are in the right place, and this is the right place. The right place for magic, if that's what you want. You have made *your* choice.'

2

At Maxim's

'I'M THE SEVENTH son of a seventh son,' he said. 'And that's something special, really special, but I didn't know that when I was little and lived in an ordinary house in a really boring street, just a boy next door.'

'But with green hair.'

I looked him in the eye. Magic, he was going to tell me about magic and I had made my choice. I'm not someone who changes her mind, not where witches and magic are concerned.

'Green hair,' I reminded him.

'What are you talking about? You see plenty of that around. Here there and everywhere – green hair, but nothing quite like mine because of the salon I go to where they do the best job in the world and what style! The place is lit by luminous toads who bounce around like nobody's business. There is no other light at all—so you better not upset the toads who will go into a huddle, if they get their feelings hurt, leaving you in the dark to have your beauty seen to in a way you won't forget—not this side of history. I have seen people leave that salon ashamed of the day they were born. Witches, hobgoblins that sort of folk, with hairstyles they hadn't bargained for and precious bits of themselves in unexpected places, like eyes in their tummies and mouths on their toes. Because that's what can happen when it goes dark in that salon where witches come and go. The queen of witches sits as still as a statue to have her beauty seen to—if you can call it that—and hobgoblins become silent because they are as vain as panthers and want a good job done. But I am glad you like my hair.'

I couldn't take my eyes off his hair. It wasn't the colour and it wasn't that it shone in the dark like the toads in all their glory; it was the feeling that came from looking at it that I couldn't get enough of. It just looked like it might always stay *the same*. Not like everything else, which might vanish or change any moment. You can't be sure of anything—not in the land of magic.

'I've always had green hair,' he said, as if he could read my thoughts. 'There have to be some things that just stay the same, though that's not what everyone thinks. Take my mother. She was a teacher. Mrs Rainbow, they called her, because of her hair. She was a witch of course, but no one knew that, except Humphrey the cat.'

'A good witch?'

'It's not that simple—not with witches. Hobgoblins,

now there you do have the good, the bad and the ugly, but not with witches. With witches, wickedness comes and goes and everything is full of surprises.'

'I have a list,' I said.

'Forget lists, just forget any kind of list. Let's talk to my mum, Mrs Rainbow. She is there on the wall and she is at the beginning of our story anyway.' He pointed at a huge picture. I got up and noticed that I'd been sitting on a slug that unfurled the stalks of its eyes, unharmed. I watched it sliding away under an old table.

Mrs Rainbow was wearing a black cape with silver moons and she had two silver stars in her ears. Her hair was bright orange with odd bits of blue.

'Don't blame me for anything or everything,' she said in a shy voice which drifted round the room and was followed by an attempt at a smile. She was in a huge black frame and seemed to be feeling the weight of it

'Take me down,' she said. 'I want get out of this frame. It gives me the creeps and you know it.' She lifted a hand covered in bangles, thin and fat ones with black and red stars, bright yellow moons and a few snakes too. 'Just take me out and we can go to *Maxim's All Night Diner*. I haven't been there for ages and I am full of longing for the place.'

'That's my mother,' sighed Patrick. 'She never told me she was a witch until it *was* almost too late. I had to do the great escape all on my own.'

'All boys have to grow up,' said Mrs Rainbow leaning out of the frame. 'They do, you know. You can't tell them everything—they have to do some of the learning themselves. And magic is something you only get to know slowly because it's an art. Who is that girl there?' She had jumped out of the frame and was looking at me in a way I didn't like.

'She's called Annabel,' said Patrick.

'That's a really, really ugly name.' She shook her arm at me and laughed. 'How wonderful and promising. How glorious and simply fantastic. I know seventeen Annabels, two hobgoblins, three spiders, a beetle, a frog and a lioness who loves clocks. It has a thing about clocks, does this lioness, and she's stealing them all the time.' For a moment she was silent and thoughtful. 'Let me think, there are also two owls, but the rest are witches—none of them very *good* witches, mind you. But still you made a reasonable choice of name. What are you writing about?'

'Witches,' I replied. 'You're my first one. I am writing down everything you are saying. And I am doing a drawing.' I should never have said that. Never. But it was too late. If you write about witches or draw them, then you must do it very secretly. You can't just sit there with your pen and paper. But how was I to know that? Not long ago I had been sitting on a bus dreaming about witches and the world of magic and now I was talking to a real one, or so she said.

'Keep your pen and paper hidden. Put it deep in your pocket,' whispered Patrick.

'Too late,' cried Mrs Rainbow. 'Much too late. My curse is upon you. The curse of a wicked, wicked witch.'

'Please,' I begged.

A sudden gust of anger seemed to sweep up the lines in her face and tie them into a knot. The tunnel of her mouth was full of sound. What a sight!

'Never use that word with witches. Never! Never say that horrible, vile, foul, abominable word. Not to a witch. I wouldn't say *please* even to a snake or a wizard, and they're not choosers, not in my books. So you can have my curse, and there's no getting round it. Hardly off the bus and in the land of magic, and already you're cursed. Takes some doing. You can have one of my special ones.'

She winked. From inside one of her huge sleeves, she took out a small ball of paper and unrolled it. She looked at it carefully.

'You will never be able to escape. Not unless you find sixteen Annabels. Now that's a tall order—one of the tallest I've ever known. You'll need more than luck. You'll need a wizard or two and they're difficult to find. And then they can't be trusted and might land you right in the mud, real deep and as stuck as an eel in a post box.'

She tore up the paper and threw it into the air and it vanished. I stood there and didn't move, my eyes on Mrs Rainbow. She was all smiles now and pleased with herself, standing proudly in the middle of that room, plants rising from the floor all around her, hurling strange flowers into the air, as if a piece of the jungle had sneaked in and was lording itself in that damp place. A small monkey lowered himself delicately by holding on to the rim of a huge trumpet shaped white flower and made himself comfortable in her hair. She kept smiling and didn't move.

'You will have to search high and low,' she whispered dreamily. The monkey blew me a kiss. 'Ever so low. See, I have given you a hint there because I am not that wicked. All those many years of teaching have taken the edge off my wickedness—all those class rooms and all that Geography. Too much Geography. Too much for my poor brain. Not that witches can't teach anything, they can *and* they *do*. But Geography is a favourite choice and I was a dab hand with maps. But that is all over now; the sweat and the tears. And now my son, we must be off to Maxim's where you can tell her the story of the great escape. Anyone who wants to know about witches will want to go there.'

She took me by the hand and and we ran through the house. My legs were cutting through the sinewy tendrils of all those plants and I could feel that they were bleeding, but I didn't care. This was what I had been waiting for.

'At *Maxim's All Night Diner* you can see more witches than can possibly be good for anyone,' whispered Patrick.

'Anyone, ever. But you *said* you wanted to meet some real witches. Boy, are there some witches and trolls there. So real, they'll take your breath away.'

We reached the door in no time and ran through the garden, jumping over a fence. A wood lay in front of us, a maze of trees and dappled light. They were holding my hands, one on each side. We were slowing down. The wood felt endless. I couldn't see any paths.

'Maxim's,' I whispered out of breath, 'are you taking me to Maxim's?'

They just kept walking, as if they hadn't heard.

'Who is Maxim?' I asked.

Mrs Rainbow stopped for a moment and looked at me carefully.

'He's the most awesome troll that ever was. What a place he runs! Every witch in the world wants to go there so it's just a golden piece of luck that you met me.' She squeezed my hand very tight. The trees were so close together that soon were were walking among dark shadows and I had no idea how they could find their way. Patrick kept telling me about Maxim's Diner.

At Maxim's there were huge chandeliers that threw balls of light on a floor full of stories. At first, all you could see was a fantastic pattern of coloured stones and shells. But then, as you looked very carefully, the patterns became people and strange creatures.

'The more carefully you look, the more you see. The stories are not easy to follow because at Maxim's familiars are welcome and the floor is covered with them. Cats of all sizes. Shy ones and awesome ones, looking for trouble like their owners. But there are not only cats: there are mice, frogs, toads, snakes too. Anything in fact, as long as it's not too big. All kinds of creatures can become familiars. Some of them will sit quietly. Some just won't. At Maxim's talking's the game, the thing to do; that and eating. The waitresses have red eyes from always being on the go. And on skates too—but even on roller skates, serving everyone is real work. One of them is always whooshing past you, tray balanced on fingertips, things spilling right and left. And the shouting just goes on and on. People snap their fingers, call out. Everything to attract attention and the waiters and waitresses come and go, banging down their trays, now at this table now at that. When they get *really* angry, they'll take their trays and crash them on the head of whoever is shouting the loudest.

'Enough,' they will say, trays crashing. 'That's enough.'

That's a risk we all take. Every so often, a whole gaggle of waitresses will surround someone with their trays and just keep bashing till a wicked squealing is heard and there is nothing left of the person at all. Just a pile of trays. It's such an awesome place.'

He had sneaked down into the kitchens several times.

No one ever noticed him; they were so busy. There he had seen huge stoves spitting fire, the shadows of the flames leaping high and dancing against the walls. The cooks shovelled pots across the hobs with lightening speed. Bright fires licked the black sides of pots filling the room with steam and wonderful smells. It was difficult to not just close your eyes and imagine yourself all nose and that's what he sometimes did. He could sit for hours underneath one of the tables, just breathing in the air of toasted frog and caramelized onions mingled with a thousand other things he couldn't name. The cooks were always busy tasting, stirring and slamming on lids. The orders were always coming in thick and fast. Everything ordered in the huge hall above was made just there and then, except the soups and the sauces. They were boiling away in cauldrons at the far end of the kitchen. The sauces were made by bats and the air was full of them. The steam would lift the lids off the cauldrons, the bats would quickly pour in herbs and oils from glass beakers, they carried in their feet.

'This is the kingdom that Maxim the troll rules,' said Patrick. 'He gives an order here, holds back there. He is in total control and enjoys that whirlwind of fire and steam in the kitchen. In the diner above, we can all hear his laughter. He is a huge hairy troll and wears a waist-coat and short trousers that finish just below the knee. He's barefooted and can be as swift as a tiger when he wants to get somewhere. In his waistcoat pocket he keeps a big watch on a long chain. Every quarter of an hour he takes it out and shouts the time. One of the cooks then takes a spoon and bangs a cauldron so that the bats all fly up to the ceiling in a cloud. He is an old troll is Maxim, but you can't mess with him.'

'At Maxim's All Night Diner no one talks quietly,' said Mrs Rainbow. 'And no one listens to anyone else for long without interrupting. Everyone wants to have their say. Stories just grow and grow. There is never much agreement. It's difficult to know what to think because witches, familiars and goblins have very strange memories and some of them tell outright lies, just for the sake of it. And their tempers are fierce.'

Finally, we were there. I could see the place right in front of me, a huge sign in curling letters, I was too excited to be afraid and I was thinking to myself, 'Just go for it, Annabel. Just go for it.'

Maxim's All Night Diner.

I couldn't wait. All that energy. All those strange creatures, I was sure to find. I really wanted to dive into all of that, but I knew that there would be danger too. Not the sort I was used to. With witches, wickedness just comes and goes, Patrick had said, meaning you never know where you are. I couldn't help feeling that went for everything in

Maxim's All Night Diner. It would be brimming with magic. All those guys so used to magic... but maybe some of them wouldn't be quite in control of things. Magic can get its own back on you, if you're not careful. That's something, I've known for a long time. Magic is dangerous. It can be like playing with fire. Real fire.

'You'll never forget a visit to Maxim's,' said Patrick thoughtfully. 'No one ever does. But remember what I said before. It's too late now and you can't go back. You'll have to join in and become part of that awesome crowd at the diner. But you can't just go with the flow— that's a loser's game and you can't be a loser. Not here. Terrible things happen to losers round here.'

I nodded looking him straight in the eye, but I could feel a trickle of sweat running down my arms.

We made our way in. Behind the door, a dark red curtain hung in folds so thick you could get lost in them and it took us some time to battle our way through. Suddenly, there we were at Maxim's. Mrs Rainbow led us straight to a gaggle of witches seated round a table talking stories. They were old fashioned stories some of them, and they were taking a detailed interest. I just let my ears pick up a few things, while I found my bearings.

'Fee-fi-fo-fum—nah he never said that—he was the silent sort, that giant with the bean stalk.'

'What do you know, what do you know about giants? Anyway, they are queer fish and totally unpredictable.'

'Fish that reminds me,' said one of the witches in an excited voice. 'Know the story of the talking fish and the giant? It's a good one. I know what you are all thinking. You are all thinking, "I know that story. Know it well. Why, it's as old as the joke about the chicken and the road. Why did the chicken cross the road? To get its own back on a toad." In the story you know, this talking fish gives the giant a wish because he doesn't eat it and just puts it back in the river, as if he didn't care where his next supper was coming from. So this fish gives him a wish. The giant wishes he wasn't a giant but an ordinary prince, married to the princess down the road. But I know a different ending, a better one and the real one. In my story the fish marries the giant, lives happily ever after and puts the princess in a dungeon. Now what do you say to that?'

No one had time to say anything because three waitresses came rolling along on their skates and banged down their trays. Immediately everyone was reaching down for whatever they wanted. At Maxim's All Night Diner no one is polite and no one says *please*.

'Well it's a good story,' continued the witch who was a very small witch. 'The rest of you don't know what you are missing. I know the fish personally and he's a very good sort, though being a fish, he does do a lot of moaning which comes from living a life in all that ocean.' She sighed and reached out timidly for a very flat grilled frog.

'Burnt, just my luck. What is happening to Maxim's?'

'Shhh,' went all the others because at Maxim's All Night Diner no one ever complains. No one. Ever. That is Maxim's law. He rules his kingdom with a will of steel and it does not matter who you are. You are a guest at Maxim's and you're lucky to be there.

Mrs Rainbow smiled and patted the little witch on the head.

'We are at Maxim's now. Remember that. And who would like to be banished? Who could imagine a life without the All Night Diner? All on your own with just a familiar? No Maxim's? It doesn't bear thinking about, it really doesn't. So eat your frog and let us all listen to the *Three Pearls* or *How to Trick a Witch* or the *Great Escape* or whatever title Patrick may choose. We will all tell a story each in honour of this girl here,' and she pointed at me. 'At the end she can chose the best one and the winner will get something really, really wicked of her own choice.'

'Everyone ready?' asked Patrick. 'Everyone ready for the story of the three pearls?'

All around us witches were banging their spoons on the table.

'Ready!' They shouted. And from table to table the cry travelled till everyone in Maxim's All Night Diner was shouting and banging. The waitresses and the waiters joined in the game by throwing their trays up into the air and catching them. Food went flying everywhere. Familiars, big and small, made a scramble for it. Finally, Maxim himself appeared.

'I will not miss a good story,' he roared. 'So let us begin.'

'It's good when Maxim is here,' said the little witch thoughtfully. 'Otherwise there are too many interruptions and you never get to the end of anything.' She had a very long pointed nose, rather fine and elegant in fact. I had thought that all witches had horrible noses and I couldn't take my eyes off her wonderful red hair that covered the table like a wave of the sea, but no one took any notice of it. They just put things on top of it and sometimes they would absentmindedly wipe their fingers in it, but she didn't seem to mind or care. If she were to get up suddenly, everything would come crashing to the floor. But she hardly moved. Only her face and her eyes seemed on springs.

'Is this your first time?' she whispered to me.

I nodded. I liked her face, small like a cat's.

'Your very first time?'

Again I nodded.

'Then you'll have to tell a story. First timers always do. A story of magic and strange things happening—and they'll have to be really weird. Really, really freaky or the hobgoblins will get you. Here they won't stand for anything less than the weird and the wonderful combined with the totally amazing. Once a first timer tried to tell a story about a frog that turned into a prince. You can't imagine what happened to him. It was too horrible.' She shut her eyes and became silent.

'What *did* happen to him?' I asked.

'You don't want to know,' she said firmly. 'Stories have to be really good here. And they have to take you by surprise.'

'Yes, they have to be really good,' whispered Mrs Rainbow in my ear. She winked wickedly and I could feel a sort of coldness running up and down my spine. 'It'll be your turn soon because it's late already, and there are not that many stories to go.'

I didn't feel I had a story in me. Not a complete one

and not one that could grab this audience who seemed to be running riot. I had a few ideas, but they were out there looking for something to hold them together.

'I'm not sure, I'll be ready,' I said looking at all those tables that filled the diner, a hundred at least. Most were full of witches, but some, I noticed, had other creatures. Right behind me was a table full of wizards, all silent and serious and with a threatening air. I could hear two of them whispering about how they were going to take over somewhere, and defeat someone.

'My crew,' one of them was saying. 'My crew is the best. The very best crew that can be found, if you take the trouble to look east of the sun and west of moon.'

'I've got no issues with your crew,' replied the other. 'But have you got the magic, the magic that it takes?'

A thoughtful silence followed. I looked at the other tables and at Maxim himself. What a mighty troll. He was standing, a full eight feet tall in the centre of the room.

'I don't think I have a story for tonight.' I said.

'That is never the problem' said the witch with the red hair. 'By the time it's your turn, you'll find that things are happening. The stories happen as you tell them. It is just a question of taking the right turn.' She was so eager she was out of breath. 'It's like this: if you take the wrong turn in your story, then hobgoblins will get you. If you take the right turn, then you may even become queen.'

At this thought she became so excited that she began to shake her head, upsetting all the things that were on her hair. Goblets of wine, plates of food, and a few of the lesser familiars. Frogs and crickets, that sort of thing. The frogs jumped into the air, food and wine rained down on the table, but the little witch took no notice at all.

'Imagine that,' she said dreamily. 'You might become queen—queen of all the witches in this world and the other one. The one that is east of the sun and west of the moon, where even more magic is known. That's a scrumdidleumcious and glorious thought, but it has never happened, you know. Not yet. For that to happen, your story has to be utterly fantastic. Completely and utterly, no room for doubt, the cough of a snake or the wink of a frog. No, everyone must agree, and *then* you become queen.' She closed her eyes. '*The Queen of Witches*. I can imagine *you* as that. Yes, there's something special about you.'

I wasn't feeling so sure.

'Silence,' shouted Maxim waving his big hairy arms. 'It is story time now. Anyone who can't sit still or be still, can leave the Diner. If the silence isn't eerie, you will all be in trouble and that includes you.' And he pointed at the little witch with red hair. 'So I will have a scrumptious, delicious, auspicious, eerie silence full of flim flam and foreboding and not a screech must be heard. And now for the story of *The Three Pearls*—I hope you remember every word perfectly. I will have no ahem, aha. And no silly detail, any 'and he had mud between his toes' and the hobgoblins will get you, because I'm not a patient giant. Stories are the best thing in the world, but some really do get on your nerves.'

'I am ready,' said Patrick looking just little pale.

'So am I.' And Maxim sat down and the diner went silent. It was as eerie a silence, as any I have ever known. I sat there and listened, knowing it would be my turn soon.

3

The Three Pearls

'THE FIRST TIME I met the *Queen of all Witches* was many years ago,' said Patrick. I was an ordinary boy back then, and I was living in an ordinary house and I didn't know that my mother was a witch. I thought she was a teacher. You all know my mother, Mrs Rainbow. When I was little, I thought that she was just mad in the way that lots of teachers are. That very ordinary madness that grabs teachers after a while and never really lets go of them. They take to shouting when they shouldn't and think that they know far more than they do about the world. They don't seem to mind what other people may be thinking of them. I thought my mother was mad in that very ordinary way. Then one day one of her friends came to visit. I can't remember what she looked like, she was that ordinary.'

'Ordinary, my hat,' interrupted Mrs Rainbow. 'Rachel Grimshaw who always wants to be different. Why, she keeps a snake as her familiar.'

'A very dopey snake called Toby. She never stops talking to it and it gives you the creeps. She *looks* ordinary but that's all. As soon as I saw her talking to that snake, she keeps in a basket, all padded as if it was some kind of precious doll—and that's how she talks to, it as if she was a girl with a doll—I decided that I would rather go to my room and be on my own. Madness is best avoided. But then I looked out of the window and I saw *it*. I saw Toby sliding slowly through the grass. He had a silly pink hat on his head. She didn't just talk to him, she dressed him. I rushed down the stairs but quietly, no banging of doors, so that no one would hear me and I followed him. I followed the snake and that is the beginning of the story. There was something weird in the way I *had* to follow that snake. He was sliding along like lightning, and I ran faster than I have ever done before. At times I couldn't see him, and all I followed was that silly pink hat. Keeping up with him, I had no time to look around me. I didn't see where I was going. I could feel my face and arms being struck by brambles and I could feel that I wasn't running on a road or a path, but all I could think about was how to keep up with that snake. I mustn't lose him. It really felt that my life depended on it. Suddenly I noticed that he was gone, and I was standing in front of a castle. It was night.

I don't know whether you have ever experienced fear.

Fear roots you to the spot, and you see things in a way you never have before. I have tried moments that had more fear in them than I had thought possible. And then you know, in that awful way of knowing things, that the worst *can* happen, and that it might happen to *you*.'

Patrick was looking at me as he spoke. He winked and that wink reminded me that I wasn't safe. Not safe at all. I wondered if I would ever be safe again. The land of magic is awesome. There was a whispering behind me and I could hear the wizards talking and exchanging secrets in low voices. Maxim looked at them sternly, his thick black eyebrows like a couple of cat's tails on his face. There was anger in his eyes. Patrick went on with his story.

'That was what I was feeling, that feeling of fear. And I was looking at *her* castle with all that darkness slung around it. *Her* darkness. The darkness seemed to be moving, making way for that queen of the night who was coming down the path in search of something, with a crowd of small men dressed in red tip toeing behind her. Red shoes with golden buckles and their feet weaving the air, as if afraid of touching the ground. You could tell she had a wicked temper.

'I told you,' she was saying. 'I am feeling evil. Very, very, evil.' She held up her hand demanding silence. 'And when I'm feeling evil, then there is no telling what I might do. No telling at all.'

'The last time,' whispered one of her followers to himself, 'the last time was a disaster. What does she mean, no telling?'

'As if *you* could have done any better,' interrupted the queen sharply. She was one of those who can hear a bat move.

'Pardon me, Majesty, but it couldn't have been any worse.'

'Give me a rose,' shouted the Queen of Witches at the top of her voice, pointing at the fellow who had spoken. He was smaller than the rest and had these nice pointed ears and a funny nose and I could see that he was *smiling*. He was the smallest and the last and he looked straight at her. The others were looking out at the darkness with their fingers in their mouths, biting their nails.

'Give me a rose, blockhead. Give me a rose, stupid. Give me a rose before I have time to think and that will be all the worse for you. When I think I can be evil. And when I'm evil...'

He handed her a rose.

'And when I'm evil ...when I'm evil ...' She stopped, she hesitated. I was sitting there, hidden in some bushes, finally daring to breathe while the moon decided he'd had enough and slid behind a cloud. The darkness was total, but they continued talking.

'And when I'm evil—when I'm evil.' She was getting herself really worked up. 'When I'm evil, I am...I am...'

'A perfect disaster, Majesty. A perfect disaster. But you can be very wicked. *Very, very* wicked.'

A silence followed. Suddenly she started shouting.

'Throw him in the dungeon. Grab that little boy who is sitting in the bushes listening. I can't bear children listening in bushes. They ought to have their heads chopped off.'

Before I had had time to think or run away, they had grabbed me.

Two of them had taken hold of me. One for each arm. They were dragging me along the path down towards the castle. As I was pulled along, I could see the wicked witch in front of me, her black cape trailing the ground like a pool of darkness. She was walking very quickly and we couldn't keep up.

'Your Majesty,' shouted one of them terribly out of breath. 'Please, Your Majesty, which dungeon?'

'Does it matter? He won't like any of them, but serves him right for spying.'

'We can't just put him in any dungeon. We won't know where to look when you want him.'

'Want *him*?' She turned round to look at me. 'Want *him*? Well, I suppose I might. I'm always changing my mind. Any good at jokes? What did the big anteater say to the little anteater? Can't answer or won't answer? There is a big difference you know, between can't and won't and I have got no time for *won't answer*. No time at all. Which one is it then, can't or won't?'

'Don't know.'

'What an idiot, what an infuriating good for nothing, empty headed fool of a boy. Put him in a hundred and forty-three. There is someone there already to keep him company. Otherwise he'll die of fright immediately and we can't have that. Brings bad luck, it does, just like a broken mirror, but not *seven years* bad luck, just a little bit of bad luck, like a lost button or a yucky runny egg for breakfast, or a dead mouse in your favourite pair of shoes, or a grumpy hedgehog in your bed. That sort of thing. An everyday sort of thing, like a flamingo in your fridge eating all your cheese without warning. Or a penguin in the freezer gobbling up your ice cream so that when you go down late at night just wanting a little something—well it's all gone. All you're left with is a penguin with a secret smile on his face filling up your freezer. God, things really *do* drive me mad! One hundred and forty-three it is. Off—march. And don't lose the key like you did last time or he'll turn into a skeleton and I'll hang him in my garden where the skeletons dance in the wind.' And she laughed her wicked laugh.

I've got to know a lot of dungeons and a hundred and forty-three is one of the worst. The dungeons in this castle were carved into the ground, so to get to a hundred and forty-three we had to go down at least a thousand steps. As we did, the place got darker and darker and more and more ghostly. About half way down, the two men who were holding me stopped to have a rest.

'Have a biscuit,' said one of them who I recognised as the guy who'd had the guts to speak to the queen. He took a grubby bag of biscuits out of a rucksack, I hadn't noticed, and sat down on a step. His hands were huge and hairy but the rest of him was quite small. I suppose he must have been a kind of goblin, or dwarf.

'My name is Soap,' he said. 'And that is Toothpaste. The wicked queen, who is also a wicked witch, calls us that to *really* wind us up. And it is pretty annoying as you can imagine.'

'I don't mind,' said Toothpaste feebly. 'I really don't. I'm past caring really. I've seen so much in my time. Boys turned into toads, girls turned into slippery slimy things, like eels and slugs and the *rest of it*. There is no telling what's next. Does your nut in after a while, it does. Why only the other day ...'

'Shut up,' said Soap. 'Shut up and eat your biscuit. Don't *you* listen to that drivel, Patrick. Just remember: you're the seventh son of the seventh son, but don't you tell anyone that. Not until you *have* to. Not until you are in *mortal* danger.'

That was the first time I heard those words *mortal danger*. And I knew immediately what they meant: danger of death.'

Patrick paused. The silence was awesome. *Mortal danger*, he had said. Those words had a queer taste.

'Mortal danger,' repeated Patrick continuing with his story.

'Is there a lot of it around?' I couldn't help asking, my heart in my mouth.

'A lot of *what?*'

'Mortal danger.'

'Loads of it. It is here there and everywhere, and you never know when you are going to come across it. But never forget that you are the seventh son of the seventh son. And that's why you are *here*. No one comes *here* by *accident*. I can tell you *that*.'

As he spoke, he shone his light on some steps carved out of mud and stone that seemed to go on and on, a never ending circular staircase that had become rock solid from just standing there in the silence underground. The shaft seemed to grow as our globes of light moved forwards. We had stopped talking and all I could hear was our echoing steps.

Finally, we stopped. 'We have arrived,' said Soap sadly giving me a hug. 'Time to enter that dungeon.'

I shall never forget first seeing that place and hearing that door close, but immediately I sat down I heard a voice and the sound of someone making themselves comfortable, if one can use that word.

'I can smell a boy,' said the voice. 'A silly little boy. The wicked witch hates boys. Don't ask me why. Anyway, I was just about to tell myself a story to put myself to sleep and you can listen too, if you want. It's a beautiful story. I heard it from the old man of the sea who lives in a cave with his fifty daughters and two sons. He's a sea-god, one of the lesser ones, but a wonderful story teller. That was a long time ago. His children were listening too, sitting all around him in the sand dunes. Each one of them was holding one of those pets, he'd given them. Penguins and crabs and that sort of thing because the old man of the sea thought pets were good for children. 'Keeps them out of mischief and teaches them about life,' he used to say. Whether that is true I've no idea, having never had pets or children myself. Anyhow, I can tell you the story which is called *The Three Pearls*.'

'Who are you?' I asked. His story didn't sound like my kind of story, but you'll talk to anyone, if you're sharing a cell.

'I'm *Sinbad the Sailor* and I've done the Seven Seas, and a lot more than that, I can tell you. I'm Sinbad and everyone has heard of *me*.'

Well, I hadn't. I had never heard of that guy at all, but I thought it best not to tell him. Later he told me that he was in some of the stories called *A Thousand and One Nights* and that some of those tales were true. Others were awesome lies, of course. Like some of the stories we tell here.'

Patrick fell silent for a moment, but Maxim roared. 'Get on with it! Just get on with it. It's a good story, though I've heard it before.'

Then, to my surprise, he came over to our table. Now he lowered his voice which would otherwise have blown me away.

'He's over there. Sinbad is over there. Can you see him Annabel?' And then he picked me up. Picked me up and held me in his hairy hand. I had never been held by a troll before. Never. What bigness! After all that's happened, I am still not happy in the company of witches—no, you never quite get used to that, but the bigness of trolls, now that's something else! It's got a purpose and just feels so natural. Most trolls are big. And Maxim is a giant *and* a troll of a very special kind. So I stood there, as tall as tall on his big hairy hand, proudly surveying the scene and feasting my eyes on this crazy company of drifters, this wave of creatures who *knew* magic, dark secrets and things, you didn't dare dream of. There, sitting between a goblin and a dragon, I could see the man they called Sinbad. On his head he wore a hat shaped like a ship. I recognized him at once. He was the man with the hats I had met in Patrick's house what seemed like ages ago.

'Time to continue with that story,' shouted Maxim

putting me down. 'Time to get on, or the hobgoblins will get you.'

'Sorry, Maxim,' said Patrick laughing nervously. 'I was just remembering the first time I met Sinbad. You all here know Sinbad, and I'm not the only one he's helped. No, a fair number of us owe more than we perhaps like to admit to his cunning and his calm. Yes, he knows how to do the right thing, and when it's the moment for it. Most of us only do that some of the time. He can move like a cat, but his face is like a worn rock. I've seen him, elbow on thigh, resting that rock of his in the palm of his hand, not moving till some stray thought makes him smile. Well, I was sitting there in that dungeon, and if the wicked witch hadn't put Sinbad there, I wouldn't be here to day. I didn't want to listen to a story just then, I was too full of fear and too many thoughts were dancing round my head. I kept trying to think of ways of escape, but the more I thought, the worse it all seemed. The door to my dungeon, a dark thing of wood and shiny bronze, was shut. Sometimes I could hear the hollow voices of the guards and the sound of their ghostly steps coming down all those stairs that wore the darkness like a cape. Then, in a quiet whisper, Sinbad began telling me the story of the Three Pearls.

It was a story about three brothers, a good brother, a bad brother and one who was so utterly wicked he didn't know night from day. Their names I've forgotten, but all three wanted to marry a princess who was locked in a tower by her wicked stepmother. Every day the stepmother would sit in front of the tower playing cards with a dragon-in-waiting. Only by making the step-mother and the dragon fall asleep could you reach the princess. The bad brother thought the princess and the kingdom were his for the taking. So he came along proudly and told a very long joke about bananas and the stepmother's left eye closed. The wicked brother told an even longer joke about elephants. That made her right eye close, but then they both got eaten by the dragon who didn't fall asleep at all. But the third brother had three pearls, given to him by an old woman with one tooth who'd asked him for a sandwich. The other two brothers had walked straight past her in their hurry to get to the princess.

'Please give me a bite of your sandwich,' she begged. 'I am an old and hungry and could be your grandmother.'

'Shut up,' replied the bad brother. 'I am eating my sandwich all by myself. I don't give anything to anyone.'

'Have this,' shouted the wicked brother and threw a rotten apple at her. But the younger brother sat down by river and shared his lunch with the old woman and she gave him three pearls. When you spun the three pearls in a certain way, you could listen to all the stories in the world till you couldn't take any more. And the wicked stepmother and the dragon sat down and listened side by side. They listened for a day and a night and then sleep came over them and the good brother climbed the tower and married the princess. And at the wedding he spun the pearls and everyone sat and listened. I have heard that they are listening still, keeping the cooks and the bakers who have made the great feast waiting.

'That is the story,' Sinbad finished. 'And there must be some truth in it because I have got them here in my pocket. Right here, I have got the three pearls, a green one, a red one and a black one. And if you learn how to spin them the right way, then you can escape.'

He spun them for me and I could hear the stories whizzing past.

'You have to bend down and listen carefully,' said Sinbad. 'When you are taken to the Queen of Witches, try to make her listen to the spinning pearls while you run away.'

'But if I spin them the wrong way?'

'Why then you disappear entirely for twelve hours, but when you come back, you are just where you started. You can't move when you are invisible. Spin them one way, and you have got all the stories in the world, spin them the other, and you disappear. It's a risk worth taking to escape from the wicked queen.'

He handed me the pearls and when I looked up, he was no longer there. All night I waited, holding the pearls very tight and hardly sleeping at all. I was really careful to stay awake, although the place was as dark as could be, and the walls too thick for me to hear the song of a bird. It's a funny thing being in a dungeon. After a while your ears start to pick up all sorts of noises you never thought you would be able to hear: lizards, slugs and spiders and ravenous spooners.

A spooner is a cross between a slug and a bat and they live deep under ground which is just as well because of the horrible screeching sound they make when they talk to one another. When I first entered the dungeon there was silence, but by morning I had my fingers in my ears, and I didn't notice someone was opening the door. I felt a hand on my shoulder.

'Today you must come to the *Great Hall* where the queen is going to test you. She tests everyone. She can never have enough testing.'

He was holding a large candle in his hand that was banishing the shadows to the corners of the cell. The wax was dripping down on his closed fist, but he didn't seem to mind. He had huge eyes in an old wrinkled face, hardly any neck and ears the size of pencil cases. He was a hobgoblin, but of the solitary kind and, as we know, hobgoblins have their wits about them. He took me by the hand and led me back up the long winding stairs. Lurking among the shadows, I saw bungums still asleep and crested dragons wagging their long tails and talking softly to one another.

I hadn't noticed any of this on the way down. The whispering and the scratching sounds of clawed creatures took my mind off the queen and her wicked test.

'She will ask you three questions,' said the hobgoblin. 'The first doesn't matter at all, and she'll only smile if you give the wrong answer. The second is worth getting right, because it will put her in a good mood, and that will make a difference. But your life depends on the third. The third you have to get right or you'll end up dancing in the garden where the trees are ripe with skeletons dancing in the wind.'

'I am the seventh son of a seventh son,' I said.

'Then there is some hope.' replied the hobgoblin. 'Every thousand years or so, a seventh son of a seventh son answers the third question right and the wicked queen goes to sleep for a hundred days and there is peace everywhere. But not every seventh son can do it.'

We were close to the very top of that long, long staircase and I could see a brown rabbit standing at the top holding a trumpet to its mouth.

'We are on our way to see the Queen,' said the hobgoblin. 'Let us pass.'

'Better you than me,' replied the rabbit blowing the trumpet. 'Seventh son of a seventh son, on his way to see the Queen with no particulars.'

'What are particulars?' I asked, in case I had some.

'Don't know,' said the rabbit. 'But no one has ever got

them, because if they ever had any, they would have left them behind. That's what you do with particulars.'

'Seventh son of a seventh son,' he repeated blowing his trumpet again 'Advancing slowly, arriving just in time for breakfast.'

'What mood is she in?' asked the hobgoblin as we passed, sounding just a little anxious.

'Don't know,' said the rabbit. 'I am too happy-go-lucky to notice such things, but I would say she was in a very wicked mood—she usually is. Be like me, happy-go-lucky. You might as well, because if you don't get the third question right, she'll cut your head off.'

Again he blew his trumpet, and on we went.

We were walking along a path full of twists and turns. The landscape kept changing so that one minute we were walking through a wood, the next we were surrounding by nothing but sand. Round one bend, I saw a huge rock of ice with a couple of seals sliding down it. It was the same with the weather: one minute the sun was shining, the next it was raining, and, when you least expected it, the wind would blow snow right in your face.

'The wicked witch, the queen of all the witches that you can find, east of the sun and west of the moon, she can never make up her mind what she likes,' explained the hobgoblin. 'And so she has to change the world every five minutes and you never know where you are. Well, we are just coming up to her castle.'

A second rabbit appeared; this time he was black.

'The Queen is expecting you. In the ballroom everyone is waiting. The music is just about to start. Please follow me.'

We walked slowly up the steps leading to the mighty door of the castle which swung open as we came closer. The steps just continued, great stone steps as if the whole place had been carved out of a giant rock. On either side stood crested dragons with tall candles in their paws, covered in wax. They were standing very still like statues, but every once in a while one of them would smile. 'Remember you are happy-go-lucky.' I heard one of them whisper. 'Those words mean something,' I thought. 'First the rabbit said them and now the crested dragon. I have got those words and the three pearls in my fight against evil.'

'I have to leave you now,' said the hobgoblin as we reached a door as tall as a tower and made of dark wood and silver. There was a huge silver knocker with the head of the queen on it, but we didn't have to knock. The door just glided open. I could see a host of witches and trolls on the dance floor twirling in time to the music. I have never seen dancing such as that. A small witch grabbed me by the sleeve, pulling me along. I was clearly expected, and that was not a good feeling, I can tell you, but I didn't have time to think about that.

She led me through the throng of dancing trolls and witches, all dressed up to kill and with their eyes on impressing one another. The musicians were a mixed bag of trolls and wizards, but the drummer was a huge toad. *The Master of Ceremony* or MC was standing not far from the band. He was a really tall wizard, as tall as the mast of a ship. He stood there, calm as anything, giving orders to the sea of dancers all around him. He seemed quite strict and his voice boomed across the room. We made our way through the dancers who could not help bumping into us, but I couldn't feel a thing. It was as if they were all made of air. A sort of lightness filled them all, the good, the bad and the ugly. Even the very, very ugly. There wasn't a troll that couldn't bounce high in the air and the witches followed. I have never seen such dancing, before or since. Yes, anyone who visits the great ballroom of the queen will be amazed.

The queen sits at a great table at one end of the hall. Behind her is a huge picture of herself, surrounded by familiars. She wears the great crown of the Kingdom and her eyes have a way of looking at you which roots you in fear. She sits all by herself at the head of the table. I was offered a stool at her feet.

'You are the little boy from the dungeon?'

I nodded.

'I don't know why little boys, and girls too sometimes, fall into my kingdom. It seems a funny thing to do.'

'Yes,' I said.

'Wrong answer,' shouted the queen. 'And that was only the first question. Got you there. You will need to be better prepared for the next one, or the hobgoblins will get you, and you wouldn't want that. Not for all the tea in China. You got the first one wrong. Now be prepared for the next one. Ready?'

I didn't reply because I thought it could get me into trouble. The MC lifted his arms and the band fell silent. The trolls and witches were standing as still as statues, exactly where they were when he lifted his arms. The toad rolled the big drum.

'What's your name?' asked the queen at the end of the drum roll.

I looked her straight in the eye. 'Happy-Go-Lucky,' I replied. 'Happy-Go-Lucky is my name.'

The MC let his arms fall, the band struck up again and the dancing carried on.

Something like a smile made its way across the queen's face.

'You have put me in a better mood,' she said. 'And *that*, I can tell you, was needed. I can't stand the dancing. I sit here every time, bored to smithereens with nothing to amuse me. You must be the seventh son of a seventh son because only they have names like that. It's the right answer. Happy goes, Lucky remains, and now all advance to the third question.'

This time the MC didn't have to raise his arms. The band stopped all by itself and everyone was listening.

'Can I ask a question?'

'It is unusual,' replied the queen. 'But the unusual I can take in my stride—when I feel like it. Go ahead, ask.'

'How come have I got more in my pocket than anyone else in this room?'

'No idea. What a silly, silly question. Bet no one else can answer that question.'

The MC shook his head.

'Well, then it's no question at all, if it hasn't got an answer. And now for mine. What was there from the very beginning of time, the very beginning when we all lived in caves and didn't know what to do with ourselves, and will be there at the very end? We've all got a favourite one, and that goes for everyone, whether you're wise, foolish or really, really stupid. No-one ever gets that. You can take your time, if you want.'

'I don't need it,' I said in that eerie silence. 'I don't need it all, because I know the answer. It is stories. Stories were there at the beginning of time, in those cave dwelling days when they were almost all we had, and they'll be there at the end. There'll be someone whispering one, just as time stops, I'll bet you. And I happen to have them all in my pocket which is why I have got more than anyone else here. For I have got *the three pearls*.'

And before she had time to say anything, I brought them out and twirled them and the queen put her hand to ear and bent her wicked face so she could listen. And they all listened; even the MC and the huge toad who beat the drums were listening. And they may be listening still, but I didn't stay to find out. I ran out the door, down the stairs and past the brown rabbit who whispered, there goes Happy-Go-Lucky, good luck to him.'

'You made it,' said Maxim. 'But only *just*. Only by a whisper and a squeak, the cough of a snake, did you escape those hobgoblins. It was those wicked spooners, the *Queen of Witches* and that *Master of Ceremony* that got you through.'

He was standing among the tables, one hairy hand on his hip, and a flute in the other. He had fished it out of one of his waistcoat pockets. It almost disappeared into his fist. I was helping myself to some of the food which looked horrible, but tasted just so good. It was all fiery and crunchy and had a way of gliding through your stomach, as if your insides were being explored.

'Hey there,' said Maxim, prodding me from behind so I jumped and dropped a beetle that had been covered in seeds and dipped in something hot, sweet and strange. It had been lying there, legs in the air, with an eat-me look about it for as long as I'd been listening to the story, and now I could hold myself back no longer. I put it back in my mouth.

'Hey there, newcomer,' boomed that great big voice. 'Hey there, it'll be your turn soon and then we'll see what you are made of. Meanwhile can you play a tune?' He handed me the flute. I don't know how he'd guessed that I can play. I can do a wicked tune when I try, but at that moment I felt strangely shy.

'Get your act together,' whispered Mrs Rainbow. 'Or this place will have you for breakfast.'

'Don't be scared,' said the little witch with all that red hair. 'Fear never helped nobody, not *here* anyhow.'

I put down the beetle and put the flute to my lips. A flute can be a cold thing, but this one was cold as ice and hot as coals at the same time. I felt that I couldn't let go of it. As soon as my lips blew that snake of air that wakes the music, I heard a sound, I'd never heard before. It was no bigger than an ordinary flute, but the air danced in it and lurched forward as if it were imprisoned in some huge pipe, or rather pipes—as if I were playing a gigantic organ. Deep in a sea of sound, I closed my eyes. When I opened them again, I saw them all dancing, as they did in the hall of the Queen of Witches where a sort of lightness filled them all, the good, the bad and the ugly. Mrs Rainbow flew past me and there seemed to be drops of blood in her hair though she was smiling.

'Stop,' shouted Maxim and grabbed the flute. 'We're not there, yet. It'll be your turn all right and then you'll see. But now time for another story.'

As soon as he spoke, everything stopped and they all returned to their places. It all happened in no time. I rubbed my eyes. Everyone was seated, where they had been before, and there was a silence, full of things about to happen.

4

In Mrs Murphy's Chowder

NOW MAXIM TURNED to the smallest witch, the one with the red hair covering most of our table. Boy, was I relieved. I never wanted to touch that flute again, even if the dancing had been fantastic. I had felt the sound swirling round me, as if in a boat, surrounded by spray and storm.

'You there, witch with the red hair,' shouted Maxim. 'It's your turn now. It's a story with bells on, you keep telling me, and it better be or ...' He lifted a hand and they all looked at him, all those many witch eyes were on him. I could tell, they were all thinking about what he *hadn't* said. The words *hobgoblins* and *get you* were dancing in our heads.

'I only know one story,' whispered the little witch. 'But I'll tell it, if everyone will listen.' They all banged their tables to show how eager they were and Maxim had to make them be silent by giving them one of his wicked looks.

'Silence, not a screech, not a scream, not a word, or you will all be banished from *Maxim's Diner* and *never* allowed back. Anyone who doesn't listen, will be banished to where the cold winds howl and dance across a desert of ice and snow, and the only real company is wolves.'

That shut them up. The small witch shook her hair, sending the food flying as she rose to stand on the table, so that we could all see her.

'It is a really good story though it has got silly name, but it is, as Maxim said, a story with bells on. Bells, wheels and roller skates. It is *that* kind of story. It is called *In Mrs Murphy's Chowder*.'

She smiled, bowed, but no one dared clap because Maxim was looking at us and I knew that soon I would be standing there, trying to tell a story. The little witch stood proudly on our table looking round. Before she began, she took her long hair and tied it into a knot so that you could really see her face. She was a witch all right. She had those eyes, those witch eyes that are much bigger than ours. The colours too are clearer. Hers were a deep green, flecked with licks of brown. She kept staring at me, as if to remind me that it would be my turn soon. Her voice was surprisingly deep. it seemed to curl itself around you in the way music sometimes does. She had a good way of throwing herself into a story and taking you with her. I closed my eyes and listened.

'Mrs Murphy lived next door to us. She was very close to my mother who was a witch of the old fashioned kind. This story happened many years ago, before she became famous here there and everywhere because of those overalls which someone one day slipped into her chowder, although some say she had put them there herself. Well, we all know the song, *Who threw the Overalls in Mrs Murphy's Chowder*? Please don't sing it, because it gives me the creeps, and, by the time you have finished with this story, you will know exactly what I mean. This is a ghost story and I know that witches don't usually tell ghost stories because ghosts and witches don't get along and have a lot of differences. Well, you all know what I mean. You just can't trust a ghost, not in this world or the next, but a witch is a witch. We all know that.

Now Mrs Murphy had a lot of children, really a lot. They were all over the house and used to enjoy hiding. I don't think anyone has ever tried to count them, including Mrs Murphy herself. I used to play with the youngest whose name was Richard. He was very small, ever so small and I was quite a tiny thing myself, but everyone noticed me, on account of my bright red hair. But no one ever noticed Richard, although he had very long nose and eyes full of laughter.

We used to play in her kitchen, playing guessing games and answering questions. Mrs Murphy used to ask us questions, sums and spells, things like that. There was a serious side to her. Which spells require fresh bats wings, what to do with mouse whiskers and what is six times six, take away two?

'I am giving you a beautiful education,' Mrs Murphy used to say, but we didn't take a blind bit of notice and only answered her questions, when we felt like it. The chowder was in a huge pot and continually bubbling. I never asked what she put in it and I never looked inside the pot.

One day Mrs Murphy slammed a huge lid on the pot, wiped her big hands on her apron and put down that spoon which she was always holding.

'The will-o'the-wisps are here,' she said. 'And there's no hiding from them. They are right here, we'll just have to hope for the best.'

Some of you may never have heard of a will-o'the-wisp. Lots of people haven't and they are lucky, the really lucky ones. In those days, I had never heard of them either. Will-o'the-wisps are difficult to describe because they have many different shapes and can change their appearance. They can look quite ordinary, quite human and you may find yourself sitting opposite one, on a train or a bus. In fact, I think that most of us have been in the company of one, without knowing it. You may have noticed something a little strange, like a sudden breath of ice-cold wind. You may have looked up suddenly and noticed that the person who was sitting opposite you reading a paper, or picking his nose, doing something quite ordinary, something you wouldn't notice, has vanished. And the funny thing is that the breath of icy air stays. If that happens, then you have met a will-o'the-wisp. That icy air is the wisp and you have to very careful, because if that icy breath enters you, then you become a will-o'the-wisp and must serve in the great army of the of king of will-o'the-wisps, till he himself sets you free.

I looked round but I couldn't see a single will-o'the-wisp or anything unusual. All I could see was the cauldron with the lid slammed on. Mrs Murphy herself had vanished, but her apron was lying on the floor, just where she had been standing. Now I was quite used to that. Mrs Murphy liked to vanish and used to do it all the time; out of boredom, or when the children were out of control, and things like bed-time were taking far too long. She was an impatient soul who some times felt that she had better things to do than looking after us children. So when the mood took her, she would purse her lips, stick her nose straight in the air and concentrate on vanishing. She didn't do anything elegantly. No, but she did it, as she had been taught, and with determination. She was that kind of witch. God bless her, wherever she is now. I could tell immediately that she hadn't done her usual vanishing. No, she had disappeared and someone else had done the disappearing for her. It had all happened far too quickly. Mrs Murphy always had to think what to do and I could usually tell what she was thinking.

The kitchen was completely empty. The only noise was the bubbling of the chowder which seemed to get louder and louder till I had to put my hands over my ears. The lid was bouncing up and down; with every bounce there was steam and a sound of bubbling that was very strange, like nothing I had ever heard before. The steam came in huge puffs which curled up and round the lid, before disappearing. I couldn't take my eyes off the cauldron which seemed full of power and menace. Richard was standing just outside with the cat, Mrs Murphy's familiar. He was waving and shouting something. Finally, he turned round and started to run along the path that led from the house towards the meadow and the woods while the cat slunk back into the kitchen. Neither of us had ever been far along it and we didn't know where it went, beyond what we could see. I wanted to follow him but my eyes were on that cauldron and the steam. The noise was so terrible that I hadn't been able to hear what he was shouting. And all the time it was increasing, a deafening heavy sound that kept me rooted there. Finally, a huge billow of steam rose into the air, much higher than before. Instead of disappearing, the steam became thicker as it rose, till it looked almost solid. I thought I could see a face. Yes, it was an old man with a beard and a crown on his head, the king of the will-o'the-wisps whom they call the *Winter King*.

'Where is Mrs Murphy?' he asked and for a moment the lid stopped slamming. 'Tell her it's no good about the overalls. I just won't have it.'

I wanted to tell him that it was only a stupid song, but before I had time to say anything, he flew out of the room, trailing the steam behind him like a veil. I decided to follow him. I could see him floating towards the woods and disappearing among the trees. I didn't stop till I reached the wood itself. Just inside the wood, where there was a green square of grass, I saw Richard. He was sitting there, lost in thought, as if he were quite alone. I was very close, but he was staring straight in front of him, as if nothing was making any impression on him. A huge butterfly was on his hand. It was the colour of blood, with a crazy dark blue pattern on its wings. He was smiling at it, in an empty sort of way, and he seemed to be talking to it. He took no notice of anything else. How could anyone sit there so still when the place was alive with movement? Among the trees were the blue lights which they call jack'o-lantern because they look like floating lanterns. Every now and then, a cloud of them would float across the grass and mingle with the girls and boys who were playing there. There were more of them than I could count and they danced completely silently and their feet seemed made of air. The familiar had followed me and was keeping close to my legs. Familiars have even more than nine lives, and more curiosity than any cat, so when a familiar is scared, you *better* take notice.

They were all joining hands and dancing. Faster and faster they swirled, till the air was full of them, but Richard just sat there looking at his butterfly, as if he were all alone. The butterfly left his hand. He followed, walking straight through the dancers as if there was nothing there but air. Nothing at all. Suddenly I could hear music and it seemed to come from the Jack o'lanterns who had assembled in a corner. I picked up the familiar and put him inside my jumper, because as long as you have got a familiar, the ghosts can't get you. A familiar is too real, too real for a ghost and this is one of the reasons why witches have them, to keep away ghosts. That and to help with spells. The will-o'the-wisps were swirling along the path in a cloud and I felt that I had to follow them. I knew, without anyone telling me, where they were going. We were heading for the throne room of the king of will-o'the-wisps. He is called the *Winter King* because his throne is made of ice and his beard is full of icicles. An ice crown is on his head. His feet rest on a little ice stool. All around him there are servants trying their best to make him comfortable. Unlike the will-o'the-wisps, they have solid bodies and wear fancy clothes that you can touch. But this is only when you see them from the front. When they turn round, you can tell their backs are completely hollow and you can see through them. They are ghosts too, but they weren't born that way, like the will-o'the-wisps. No, they were ordinary creatures once: witches, goblins, hobgoblins, giants, toads, wicked stepmothers, mermaids even. The usual crowd. It's a pitiful and awesome sight and they go about their business ever so sadly because the Winter King is never, ever satisfied. There is always something wrong —horribly wrong, and there is no knowing what it might be. It could be the day of the week —the Winter King is particular about everything.

'How dare it,' he will shout. 'How dare it be Tuesday? Bring Tuesday here immediately. No sooner, *at once*. Bring in Tuesday, march him between you. Listen to no nonsense. Whatever he says, just hit him on the head with an orange or whatever comes to hand and tell him that I mean business. I want an answer and I want it from Tuesday himself. No good being shy like the other days of the week. Why is it Tuesday? If Tuesday doesn't know, who does? Answer me that if you can, you imbeciles, you monkeys, you good for nothings.'

This is the sort of thing they have to listen to, day and night. The winter palace echoes with the sound of his fiery voice asking questions. The echoes seem to chase one another through the palace becoming feebler and feebler, till all you can hear is a whisper, if you are working in the kitchen deep down below where hundreds of strange dishes and concoctions are prepared. The cooks work like devils, slamming pots and stirring cauldrons. Still you can hear the echo of the voice of the Winter King, slipping round the pots and saucers, curling like a wisp of smoke and rising in the air. If you put your ear to the wall, you can hear it quite clearly and you know it's him, because he's always shouting, *'imbeciles, monkeys, and good for nothings.'*

As I entered the throne room having crossed the great drawbridge, which is overhung with as many icicles as there are in the all of Siberia, I saw Richard. He was sitting just behind the throne of the Winter King. The butterfly was on his shoulder, so I knew that he had not yet become a ghost, because nothing real wants something unreal, unless it's doing a dance. It's the wicked dance of the will-o'the-wisps that's the fatal attraction. It's that whirling in the air, that swirling of bodies in their awesome lightness, that moving this way and that of a thousand feet or more that is bewitching. You just want to join all that movement, although you know that that there is nothing there: you can put your hand straight through all those dancers doing that wicked, wicked dance. I had followed them—but I hadn't danced. I had watched only, and so had he. What had stopped us was the butterfly and the familiar which I held close to my chest. The butterfly was as red as blood, the servants all wore mossy green, the Winter King was dressed in blue. I wore black, as we witches generally do, unless we are going out for dinner, or heading for Maxim's All Night Diner in all its glory where everyone likes to be dressed to the nines, as my grandmother used to say. Boy, did I wish myself back here surrounded by friends, in good company. But, there I was, in the throne room of the Winter King, at the very entrance to that enormous room. It was so huge that even the Winter King looked small and lost in that cathedral of ice, but you couldn't miss his roar. You really couldn't.

'Come forward. There is a witch lurking by the door. Come forward witch.'

My feet took me towards the throne. As I came closer, two servants joined me, one on either side, so I couldn't escape.

'I want to know, witch, why I am angry. Tell me.'

I didn't know what to say.

'Tell me why I am angry,' boomed the voice. 'Angry, angry,' echoed the walls. At that moment the butterfly flew up and Richard looked round. I was terrified he might realise where he was and want to join the dancers. Then he would never be able to return. I kept my eye on the butterfly. It flew up towards the ceiling and then down, landing on the Winter King himself. Suddenly I saw what was wrong. The butterfly had landed on his leg: the Winter King was in his underpants. Something was missing, and of course I remembered the old song.

It was spinning round and round in my head, '*Who threw the Overalls in Mrs Murphy's Chowder?*' I waited for him to speak again.

'Why am I angry and what do I want to know?'

'To know, to know,' boomed the walls.

'You are angry,' I said. 'You are very angry because someone has taken your overalls. And what do you want to know? Well, I think you want to know who threw your overalls in Mrs Murphy's Chowder. I can't answer that, because I wasn't there. But if you would allow me, Your Majesty, I shall dive in and fish them out. Although I am only a small witch, I am not afraid of anything. Nothing in the whole world.'

The cauldron was immediately brought in. It seemed to slide in through a door, I hadn't noticed. It was bubbling away but the steam looked cold as ice. I beckoned to Richard and we both jumped in. We jumped into that swirling mass of chowder, cold as snow, but bubbling and swirling. We were twirled round and round so fast that it was difficult to see anything. It was the strangest chowder you can imagine: full of will-o'the-wisps and dead creatures from the deep. That is why the song just gives me the creeps and I would rather forget about it. Round and round, faster and faster we went. I felt something close to the bottom of the cauldron and I held on to it. From there we were forced back up, through all that mass of chowder, till suddenly we had

reached the top and could jump out. There we were back in Mrs Murphy's kitchen. I looked at what I was holding. Well, you have probably guessed: it was the overalls. A pair of bright blue overalls. And I am wearing them now. The Winter King's overalls, as you can all see.'

At this point she pointed proudly to her chest. I had never before seen a witch in overalls but it was a good sight, I can tell you. Then we all sang the song, but she didn't join in. 'No one will make me do that,' she said. 'Not for love nor money.'

5

The Queen's Eye

'ANY OTHER STORIES?' shouted Maxim. 'I have had quite enough of all that singing and I don't want to close the Diner. The night is still young. Young for anyone who dabbles in magic like we do. The stars are still in the sky, the waiters and the waitresses are on their roller skates, ready to serve anyone who wants more food. The cooks are doing the work of the devil in the kitchen and won't be disappointed. Why, you can hear the banging and the clatter from down below. So we better have another story and I think this time a goblin or a hobgoblin should tell one because they are always complaining and moaning. No end of moaning, and I can't stand it. So we'll have a story, or they can all leave the Diner and with a flea in their ear.'

He stamped his hairy feet and the chandeliers began to wave and we could hear the cooks shouting. For Maxim is a mighty troll and there is no messing with him.

I saw a small goblin with a long beard get off his chair.

He was so small that he had to jump. His white beard reached the floor. Maxim picked him up and held him in his big hairy hand.

'So what have you got to tell?' he asked.

'The story of the queen's eye,' said the goblin proudly. He was a tiny thing, but his voice was good and strong. *The Queen's Eye* is one of the best. It is positively wicked. So wicked it takes your breath away. Be prepared.'

'Ah,' smiled Maxim, 'another one with wheels and roller skates. Worthy of my Diner. Maxim's All Night Diner. So let's begin. Now, tell me which queen are we talking about? There are so many queens. Goblins have queens, familiars have queens, and packs of cards have queens. Four I think. I lose track of all those queens.'

'Why the Queen of the Witches herself. Her wicked eye.'

'Now you are talking,' said Maxim. 'That must be a really wicked story.'

'So wicked it takes your breath away. But it begins slowly. It begins slowly and gets faster and faster and more and more wicked. So here goes.'

We were all silent. Maxim held the goblin up high so that we could all see him and his voice was, as I said, good and strong. I was feeling quite calm. It wasn't my turn for at least another story. I was beginning to get that confident feeling in my bones, that feeling that I could deal with anything. Was I wrong or was I right? I don't know, because things are still happening—still happening to *me*. You're never safe in the land of magic, I can tell you. And if you ever want to go beyond reading, to where real magic happens, then you better remember that. Safety is something, you've left behind. *You are never safe in the land of magic.* That's all that's to it. Some facts need hardly any words at all. My thoughts were chasing this and that. Meanwhile, the goblin began his story.

'Once upon a time, not that long ago really, but before anyone who is alive now was born, the sea was a much more interesting place than it is now. First of all, there were many more pirates and the sea itself was a much livelier place and you couldn't go anywhere without something strange happening to you. In those days, pirates knew what they were about, and anyone with any sense steered well clear of them. Also, it was dangerous to swim in the sea because it was full of creatures that knew magic and didn't mind doing wicked things.

In those days, which as I've said, were not really that long ago, there lived in a cave a creature called the Wask. He had one of those heads which you see on seals these days, except his nose had a bump which allowed him to wear little round glasses. He had legs and feet, but no toes, and flippers instead of hands. He had eyes which made it very difficult not to like him: very big and brown and you couldn't help noticing them because there was nothing much else in his face, except some very long grey whiskers of which he was very proud.

'They belonged to my grandfather and to his grandfather before him, you see,' he used to explain. 'And that's why they look so old. They are very ancient whiskers.'

Being just by the sea, his cave was often full of sand and with high tide the water came in. The Wask didn't mind this in the least, being a sort of walrus, but with human bits here and there. He was very nosey and used to spend most of his time looking through a very grand telescope that looked like the kind that pirates have, to keep an eye on one another, when they're sailing the seven seas. But the Wask's telescope was far better than anything an ordinary pirate would use, because with it you could see anything, you wanted. All, you had to do, was to want to see it and say some magic words.

As I said, the Wask lived all by himself on the edge of world with his telescope and lots of notebooks. He loved writing things down; all the many things he saw through his telescope, sitting there very cheerfully with his flippers in the sea, being a glorious mixture of man and beast and entirely happy with himself and whatever he was doing. He took notes on everything, he saw, very slowly, dipping an old fashioned pen in an enormous inkwell at his side, half buried in the sand so it wouldn't fall over. If anything really surprised him, he would take off his little round glasses, rub them before he started writing again and grunt or say something out loud. His cave was full of notebooks, each with its own lock, and he kept a bunch of keys in a pocket that he had tied round his waist with a string because the Wask didn't wear clothes, but he found a pocket very useful. The notebooks all had writing on their spines so you knew exactly what was in them. They were in the Wask's best handwriting which was like people used to use a long time ago, when writing was something very special.

Now this went on for a very long time, hundreds of years I suspect, for the Wask's note books stretch back almost to the beginning of magic and his cave was really a library of all the strange things that have ever happened. Why, there were books and books on witches and trolls, unicorns and familiars and that sort of thing on shelves high up on the rough walls of his cave, just out of reach of the sea. Then one day something terrible happened.

He was looking through his telescope stroking his whiskers. This was what he always did, when there was something at the end of that telescope that really made him curious.

'I'm so curious,' said the Wask. 'So curious, ever so curious. Ah, I'm deliciously, curious, wonderfully curious, splendidly curious, marvellously curious. My curiosity knows no bounds, no limits, no fences, no kingdoms. And it will never be satisfied. Never ever, because that is the kind of fellow I am: the most curious creature in the world. Pure nosiness, that's me.' He clapped his flippers together, let go of his telescope for a moment. When he picked it up again, what he saw, wasn't what he'd been looking at before. It was not, most definitely not. It was something he had never seen before. It was an eye, a single eye. And the eye was looking at *him*. It seemed to be just at the end of his telescope staring at him. A huge green eye. Nothing else. Absolutely nothing else.

'My God,' whispered the Wask. '*The Queen of the Witches*. She is here —at last.'

The eye winked and disappeared and everything around the Wask was very still, and for the first time the sea made no sound. The Wask kept looking through the telescope, and he noticed that he could now both hear and see her. What he saw was the Queen of Witches in her tower playing cards with one of her witches-in-waiting, and what he heard was, '*Bring me the head of the Wask on one of my grandmother's fancy plates. I cannot stand spies. I loathe and despise them. I've put up with that Wask for long enough. He's a spy if I ever saw one. A spy and nothing but a spy; bring me his head on a plate, but chop off his whiskers first.*' Her voice was deep and growly and you wouldn't mistake it. Even if you had never heard it before, something would tell you: this is the Queen of Witches speaking. And she is speaking to *you*.

She began to laugh. All he could see was her green eye. All he could hear was her laughter, a laughter that

seemed to fill his cave till it became a mighty roar. 'Bring me the head of the Wask,' she was saying. 'Give me the head of the Wask.'

Terrified he ran into his cave, but the eye followed him. It studied his many shelves of notebooks, bouncing up and down the spines.

'Aha,' said the voice, 'done a lot of spying have we?'

'In a way, Your Majesty,' said the Wask humbly. 'In a way. Though I didn't think of it like that.'

'Didn't think! You didn't think. What right have you not to think!'

'Every right,' whispered the Wask. 'I thought, every

right. I just look through my telescope, in the way of my father Wask, grandfather Wask and great grandfather, and great -great grandfather Wask. Every Wask since the beginning of time has been sitting on this beach with a telescope and not much else, if you'll humbly excuse us; and spying, if that's what you like to call it, spying on witches, trolls and unicorns, and all those kinds of creatures in a very peaceful way, if you don't mind my saying, a very peaceful way. I'm the first one to take notes; and they are very good notes, fancy notes, bound up and treasured, and locked away so that no one comes to any harm.'

'*Harm*, you don't even know the meaning of the work *harm*; but you'll understand it alright when your head is cut off, swish swash, and put on a plate.'

Then the eye winked, disappeared and the voice fell silent. The Wask could hear the roar of the sea again. That is when he started his journey. He took with him the telescope and a couple of sandwiches. The sandwiches he put in his pocket, the telescope he slung over his shoulder, keeping it safe with a long leather strap on which he had painted witches, familiars and unicorns in a landscape of castles, meadows and trees. It was a curious strap because if you looked at it very closely, everything seemed to be moving. The closer you looked, the more you saw, till it made you quite dizzy, and you saw things that you didn't want to see, like slithery slimy things, and the big hairy eyebrows of the Queen of the Witches, who seemed to be here, there and everywhere.

'There's no getting away,' whispered the Wasp sadly to himself. 'But I shall try. I shall try to escape that awesome queen. Perhaps her eye will just get tired of looking at me.' He sighed knowing that just wouldn't happen. Witches never tire of anything. In that way, they're different from us. Still, he had to do something.

His journey lasted twenty nights and twenty days. He couldn't stop thinking about the eye and that made the Wask very silent and very afraid. He didn't use his telescope for fear that he might see it. He couldn't stop imagining it and that, I've heard, is what usually happens to anyone who has looked straight into the eye of the Queen of Witches. The eye stays with you and you see it peeking out of bushes, or high up among the branches of trees, or even, occasionally, skimming the surface of the moon, as if it were a cloud being pushed along by a sudden and angry burst of wind. It's not a good state of affairs and does funny things to your brain, being watched like that by someone who is, and isn't there. I've tried it myself, I can tell you, so I know what the Wask went through on that cold journey with its dark nights. He carried a lantern, but of the kind that is always going out—because the wind is too strong, or the candle has fallen over. He felt *very* alone. His whiskers had gone grey, and he shuffled along, coughing as he went. The journey had quite taken the stuffing out of him, but he wasn't going to give in, not even to the queen.

'Damn her eye,' he would mutter to the wind, the weasels, and whatever else the night might embrace, hidden here and there, among the bushes and down holes and burrows, and all those funny places where wild things like to live and lurk. 'Damn her eye, her wicked eye and its wicked, wicked look. Why I've never seen so much wickedness, not in one place. No never. It's too much for a poor Wask. A poor, poor Wask who always *did* mind his own business, even if he did take notes. Damn her eye, her wicked, wicked eye.'

The eye kept appearing and its stare was as cold as a piece of ice, and if he returned that cold, cold stare, it would wink, rolling its lid with its black lashes very slowly as if to tell the Wask that it was having fun. She has a sense of humour does the Queen, but not one that's easy to share. It is difficult to laugh with the Queen of Witches. Very difficult. And the Wask didn't try. He just cursed that wicked, wicked eye. He cursed it as he crossed the *Plain of Trolls* with its scattered sand dunes, tall grass and hoards of familiars.

The trolls breed familiars for witches. They sell them by the dozen to gullible witches telling them that they can do this that, and the other, but it's usually a pack of lies. The familiars can't do anything much at all, except grow fat in the company of witches who don't really expect much else from them, though you wouldn't think so from their cursing and shouting and screaming and flailing of arms. The trolls are no more than two foot tall, but they are not at all frightened. They have big, round heads and friendly eyes and their laughter sounds like a warm rumble coming from their stomachs, or some-where even deeper down, seeping up through their little bodies from their big hairy feet. Witches must have familiars because there is nothing so wicked that it doesn't want company. The trolls know that. So they continue breeding these funny creatures that on the whole look like cats, but are really a race apart. They are perfect creatures for witches because they'll put up with their company, no matter what. There's no such thing as a witch that is too smelly or too peculiar, and witches can be awfully peculiar. So peculiar that it makes your head spin, just thinking about it, but the familiars don't mind. They just laugh. They have a high-pitched laughter that is somewhere between that of a human and a hyena, but otherwise they look and behave like cats, except that they can do things that cats can't do, like talk and count. Witches can't count to save their lives so the familiars come in handy when they are doing their spells and their magic and all the many kinds of badness that witches get up to. Without the familiars, the witches would be left with just their fingers and toes to count on, and that would be a sad state of affairs, and not at all easy if you want to do a spell in a hurry. However, the trolls are always exaggerating how good the familiars are at counting because, as I told you, the familiars aren't really much good at anything and so the witches are forever cursing and screaming and blaming the trolls for everything but the trolls just laugh.

We have to imagine the Wask on his journey, the telescope dangling at his side, his glasses perched on that hump of a nose, the whiskers grey and sad, and his shy sideways glance, always hoping *not* to see the eye. He would whisper and mumble to himself, as if he were all alone but the eye was always there. Always somewhere, and every time he saw it he felt a fresh jab of fear.

He could never get used to the eye and he would never have finished his journey, if he had not adopted a familiar. The creature had noticed the Wask talking to himself, as he walked across the Plain of Trolls. The trolls had taken no notice of him at all except to give him bowls of that rich, hot stew that they make and of which they're so proud, believing it to be the only thing worth eating in the whole world. In return the Wask would listen to their stories with a miserable and mournful air and allow them to play with his telescope through which they could see the most fantastic things, the most wonderful things and just what trolls like to see. They would fight one another to have a peek, while he just sat there trying *not* to look at the eye, a monstrously difficult thing to do that needed all his concentration. This familiar had been following the Wask for some days, before he noticed it one evening, as he bent down to put his spoon in the bowl of stew that was lying between his flippers going very cold. He noticed it because it was standing on its hind legs between the bowl and the eye that was lurking amongst the branches of one of those small cactus like plants that grow on the Plain of Trolls and are horrible prickly.

'Now you see *it*, now you don't,' laughed the familiar with a laugh, the Wask thought *might* be wicked. He was a small grey thing, with splashes of colour as if someone had dribbled ink on him and his hair stood up in funny tufts. He seemed the sort of fellow, you might accidentally step on, or drop something on, and he had the look of having been through something—a bush perhaps—and forgotten to groom himself afterwards.

'Now you see *it*, now you don't.' And it laughed till it had to hold its stomach with both hands and the eye bounced out of the bush and settled between its ears.

'My third eye,' it whispered between howls of laughter. 'I've got the eye between my ears.'

'You can laugh,' said the Wask sadly. 'It hasn't been persecuting you. It hasn't been after you night and day, winking and bouncing and lurking here and there and everywhere and reminding you of the Queen of Witches who is the wickedest creature in all the world. There is no doubt about it. No doubt about her wickedness and that is why I am off to see the unicorn, the one who eats magic leaves and knows everything there is to know about the big, the bad, the ugly and the really, really wicked.'

'Really?' said the familiar sounding interested. 'I would like to see the unicorn. It's certainly more fun than staying here with the trolls. Nothing ever happens here.' He looked at the Wask who was looking sadly at the ground. Suddenly the familiar grabbed the eye with one of its paws and stuffed it in a bag that he carried round his waist. His paws looked liked hands, except they were covered in fur and he had very long black nails.

'See, I'm not afraid,'

The eye bounced up and down making a rattling sound inside the bag.

'I'm not afraid of *her* eye. You can rattle as much as you wish, old eye. As much as you wish. Can I come with you? You need someone small and brave.'

That did it. The Wask had found his familiar and he called him Roland which is a very good name for a familiar and he's been known as Roland ever since. Roland the brave, as he's the only creature in the world who has ever dared to take on *Stanislaus the Wicked*. But I'm coming to that.

Roland could tell the Wask all sorts of things that he didn't know about, like who was in power and where.

'Beyond the *Plain of Trolls* lies the *Duchy of Dronymore*, an absolute hell hole of a place and I wouldn't recommend it because of the duchess, but I don't see how you can get round it if you want to see this unicorn. Let me draw you a map of the whole known world and I'll show you how to get to the unicorn, though we may not have to go that far. Not at all. You just never know what might happen.'

With a stick Roland quickly drew a map on the hard ground. The map was round like a ball. Round the rim in the top half, he wrote carefully in fancy writing. The fancy writing looked something like this: **MOUNTAINS OF FIRE.** Below he wrote **Dragons and Mountains of Ice.**

'In between the mountains of fire and the dragons and mountains of ice, there is a real hotchpotch of creatures and dangers. The mountains of fire and ice curl right round the kingdom of magic, our world. The idea is to stop anyone from outside coming in, but it doesn't quite work even if there are the dragons, and it doesn't stop witches getting out and wrecking havoc in the world outside.

'Now the Duchy of Dronymore is a really awesome place, even without the duchess who gets a new idea every two minutes and drives you mad. She's as fat as an elephant, although she was beautiful once and hasn't forgotten it. I know her familiar and he's got some stories to tell.' Roland sighed and clutched his tail. 'Anyhow, you have to go through the Duchy if you want to reach the unicorn. And if having to deal with the duchess wasn't bad enough, there is a war on at the moment. The duchess is being attacked by a whole hoard of wolards led by Stanislaus the Wicked himself and he is so bad, you might prefer the duchess.'

Roland added a lake here, a mountain range there and wrote **wolards** in big letters.

'I'm not sure,' he said thoughtfully. 'I'm not sure how you deal with wolards, or Stanislaus, but everything is possible, if you're brave.'

'With you, I can do anything. Let's set out for the land of the duchess,' said the Wask looking into his hairy face.

It took them a long time to reach the Duchy, but with Roland as a companion, the Wask was feeling good. He was even beginning to make jokes about the eye which kept bouncing up and down in the bag which Roland had tied round his waist.

Now the duchess happened to be in her garden eating a very large breakfast consisting of toast, crabs, boiled eggs and sausages. She is, as I said, abnormally fat and full of mischief and wickedness. She has five sons and three daughters who live in various parts of the Duchy and hardly ever speak to one another. They are fearfully proud and live in separate castles with drawbridges and moats and dragons. On this particular morning, they were all in the garden sitting round a very large table with the duchess at the head. The crabs were scuttling from plate to plate, bringing toast, eggs and sausages which they held in their claws. Crabs have manners wherever you go, unlike most creatures you meet, goblins and hobgoblins included. However, they do have a nasty temper, when they feel that enough is enough. The duchess and her family were all having breakfast together because they needed to make some clever plans to deal with the wolards who were marching through the magic *Forest of Id* which surrounds the duchess's castle. In the middle of the table lay a letter written by Stanislaus the Wicked. It had arrived, sent by arrow and the arrow was still stuck in and firmly attached to the table.

'Pass me the strawberry jam,' said the duchess to her youngest son who was busy trying to wrestle a sausage from a crab who had decided to hold on to it because he wanted it for himself. 'Pass me the jam, before I lose my temper. Who is that goofy fellow with whiskers who is staring at us, as if he had never before seen a family deliberating the contents of an evil letter over breakfast? Have you never heard of Stanislaus the Wicked? And if you haven't, where were you born? What planet did you last call your home? I have never seen a more bedraggled familiar. No witch would be caught dead with that piece of fluff and fur, but then you are not a witch but some kind of fish or walrus with glasses and a weird telescope and I bet it's of a magical kind that allows you to see all sorts of things. Don't deny it. You can't keep anything from me, young man. I can see straight through you. And I know what's in that bag too. It's the Queen's eye, her roving eye as she calls it because it can wander.'

They all looked at him. All five sons and three daughters, and you can imagine what *that* felt like. Not a sound could be heard, except the scuttling of crabs. They all sat there like statues while Roland helped himself to toast, jam and sausages. The Wask just stood there in a pool of thoughtful silence.

'I could help you in the fight, the great battle against the wolards,' he said finally. 'But only if you help *me*.'

'Help,' screamed the duchess picking up a crab and dipping it in the jam. 'I don't help anyone, dead or alive. I am a duchess and that means that I do what I like to do, and I am what I want to be. Why I could make myself invisible, and I could make all of you invisible but that wouldn't really help against those wolards.'

'What does a wolard look like?' asked Roland.

'Depends on the kind. These are the marching kind. They are royal wolards and have crowns on their peaked caps. They are about my height, so they are tall and elegant.'

'But vicious,' interrupted one of the daughters.

'Their faces are a strange yellow,' added another.

'And they do everything they are told and never ever stop marching.'

'They will march over mountains and over hills.'

'And they have no brain whatsoever. All they ever say is, *Yes, Stanislaus.*'

'Stanislaus is twice the height of a wolard,' said the duchess. 'And he's five times as proud. He has to conquer the duchy because he has lost his own kingdom in a game of cards. He lost that and the key to his suitcase where he keeps various things that have to do with magic. No kingdom and no magic. No wonder he is desperate.'

Roland was eating his breakfast slowly. He had a lot to think about.

'Well, your Royal Highness,' he said finally.

'Royal Duchess,' corrected the duchess. 'I am not a *highness* even if I am very high, *and* tall and mighty, although you don't really notice because of my fatness, which is a good sort of fatness. You could do with some yourself, if you don't mind my saying so. You are the saddest familiar, I have ever seen. Why, you look like you have been sleeping in a ditch or two.'

'Or three or four,' interrupted one of her daughters.

'Be quiet,' said the duchess. 'This is no time to be talking about ditches. This familiar has something about him which is more than you can say about that goofy fellow with whiskers who does nothing but stand there. Hey there, want some breakfast? If you want any, you better help yourself, before the crabs retire for the day, leaving us with no service.'

The Wask sat down shyly at the table and the crabs brought him a roll and jam and butter.

'I'm on my way to see the unicorn,' he explained. 'He is going to help me get rid of that beastly, wicked eye, but meanwhile I am happy to help. My name is Wask and I am the most curious creature in the whole world, and just for that the Queen of Witches wants to chop off my whiskers and have my head on a plate. Her eye has followed me across the Plain of Trolls to your duchy, both through night and through day. Finally, we put it in a bag, but that hasn't really helped because it bounces up and down and sings songs during the day and tells ghost stories at night. I'm in despair but this Roland is braver than me and just answers back. He knows of ghost stories that can make the eye blink and tremble, like the one about the seven headless wonders who used to live on the moon and rattle their chains and play cards and tricks on one another. Or the dragons who live by a blue lagoon and are just full of magic to bursting.'

'I don't doubt that this Roland knows a thing or two,' sighed the duchess so loudly that a couple of crabs jumped off the table. 'But can he get rid of wolards, marching wolards? You can even hear them right now.'

And suddenly they could all hear the sound of trumpets and voices singing, '*Wolards forever*' and '*long live Stanislaus the wicked, wicked, wicked.*'

'Listen to that,' said the duchess wrinkling her nose. 'Well Roland?'

Roland didn't say a word, though all eyes were upon

him. The duchess was looking at him; the five sons and three daughters couldn't take their eyes off him. They were sitting as still as still while the march of the wolards could be heard getting louder and louder.

They closed their eyes almost expecting to be swallowed up by the boom, boom of the marching feet. Roland brushed a few crumbs from his face. Finally, he spoke.

'I shall play him at cards,' he said.

'What?' shouted the duchess. 'You shall do what? You will play who at cards?'

'Stanislaus the Wicked. I shall play Stanislaus the Wicked himself.'

The five sons and three daughters banged the table and started shouting, but no one was listening to them.

'Silence!' screamed the duchess, 'I will have silence. Now this familiar, this little familiar with the funny fur and green eyes has got something. He hasn't got the finest tail or the best pair of whiskers in this duchy, but he has got brains. Brains and courage. And I know what I am talking about, for I have been a duchess for over a hundred years and I have seen a thing or two in my time. Well, if you succeed you shall have the highest order in the land and you can wear it on your chest with pride.'

Now there is nothing that familiars like more than fancy medals. I am sure you have noticed that in the annual witches' parade when familiars and witches walk proudly together, carrying their banners so that you know which coven they're from, those familiars, who have orders or medals, really strut and look quite ridiculous. Or so it would seem to a goblin like myself. For we goblins and hobgoblins are creatures of a solitary kind and we don't much care what other people think of us. Roland had his eye, his beady eye on the order of the *Golden Sock and Stars* which no familiar had ever worn before.

Meanwhile the sound of the wolards stamping and singing could be heard and quite a racket it was. The ground was beginning to shake.

'The Golden Sock and Stars,' muttered Roland. 'I won't do it for anything less.'

'You have got your wits about you,' replied the duchess. 'And that deserves something.' She stroked him gently because he belonged a bit to the cat family and was quite soft, if wild to look at.

Suddenly an arrow with an envelope attached to it whistled through the air and landed on the table right in front of the duchess. She took out the arrow and opened the envelope. It carried the seal of Stanislaus, a skull and cross bones because his ancestors used to be pirates, or so he claimed to give the impression that he was someone born into wickedness of a hell raising kind.

'I *Stanislaus the Wicked*,' read the duchess slowly, '*hereby proclaim, announce, shout and declare that the Duch-*

ess of Dronymore has no Duchy anymore, none to speak of, because I, the aforesaid Stanislaus, am busy occupying it with my wolards and wrecking havoc. You might as well, dear Duchess...'

'He has some nerve,' whispered the duchess, 'calling me 'dear'. No one has *ever* done *that* before.'

'*You might as well, dear Duchess, throw in the towel. I know it is difficult but the time has come to bow to the might of Stanislaus. So I humbly suggest, and with some respect, for never was there a finer or fatter duchess, that you accept what must happen. To be brief: you should throw in that towel and get a new life. It's been done before. I believe your great-grandmother did something similar. Signed in blood, faithfully yours, Stanislaus. Ps: will be with you any minute. Don't move.*'

'What did your great-grandmother do?' asked Roland.

'Married a one eyed dragon who blew fire all over the duchy. It was a last resort. I don't intend to do that. I won't marry Stanislaus, should he have the nerve to ask. Not for all the magic in the world. He seems to be dropping some kind of hint, but I am turning a very deaf ear. And the rest of you better do the same.'

'Don't worry,' said Roland in a very respectful voice, the voice of someone who can already see himself wearing the *Golden Sock and Stars*. 'This Stanislaus will regret that he ever entered the Duchy of Dronymore. Wask, give me your telescope. I need it.'

'No, you don't,' said the Wask sadly. 'It is completely

unnecessary. You don't need it because Stanislaus is already here. Right here. He couldn't be more here.'

And there he was, standing in front of a troupe of wolards puffing out his chest. Stanislaus has a very big nose, huge eyebrows and small black eyes. His hair is the colour of carrots and he wears a very large hat which he claims once belonged to someone called Napoleon. He says he is related to him, but of that one can't be sure. How can he be related to a human? On his chest is the order of the black skull, which he has awarded himself, as well as several others, some of which he has stolen. He is a regular brigand, has the mind of a pirate and a temper that would make a volcano blush and hasn't been seen this side of the moon since time began. That is Stanislaus, *Stanislaus the Wicked*. And I think we should all be glad that he is not here now, up to his usual wickedness in Maxim's All Night Diner. Well, he stood there in front of the duchess, gnashing his teeth, but not saying anything. He's not much good with words which is why I suppose he wrote the duchess a letter and sent it on ahead.

'What do you want?' asked the duchess not turning a hair. 'What can we do for you?'

She sat quite still and very like a duchess. The crabs scuttled to the top of the table and hid behind the salt and pepper. The Wask fingered his whiskers nervously and kept looking at the ground. Roland picked up a crust of bread and ate it thoughtfully.

'You have received my letter,' said Stanislaus. 'My wolards control the duchy. And they are marching wolards, so they will stop at nothing. Nothing at all. Just look at them: they can't stop marching. Why, their little feet are going up and down, up and down but on the spot because I have given orders. Orders that must be obeyed. Just look at them.' He held out his arm and pointed. 'It's a pleasure, isn't it? A pleasure to see so many wolards, so many marching wolards.'

'I would call it rude,' sighed the duchess. 'Not the sort of behaviour I am used to. I can't stand wolards, not of any kind.'

'Well,' shouted Stanislaus. 'My blood is boiling. I will not have my wolards insulted— not in any way. This is no way to speak to Stanislaus the Wicked. Do you know what wicked means? You don't know anything about wickedness, real wickedness. Your bad temper is nothing. Why you are known everywhere as the fat, bad tempered duchess, and I must say...'

He could hardly speak he was so angry. He was huffing and puffing and his face went quite red. 'I must say I am not disappointed—not in your fatness anyhow which is some fatness, an extraordinary fatness. Yes, it quite bowled me over—had me speechless, what fatness and a head the size of plate! But your temper? Not a chance there —not against my wickedness which is of the finest kind. Pure wickedness, the kind you can't learn, can't guess, and can't understand because it *must* be in the blood—in the blood, to make any sense at all.'

He was silent. It was as if he had said everything, he could possibly say. All you heard was the stamp, stamp, stamp of the wolards, the marching wolards. The duchess looked down at the crabs who were huddling closely together.

'Well,' said Stanislaus tapping his medals and fingering his hat.

'Fancy a game of cards?' asked a voice, a small strong voice. Stanislaus looked round and saw where the voice had come from. He saw a small creature, a familiar of the cat kind but standing upright, one paw holding a piece of toast and, while waiting for an answer, it continued to *eat*. Stanislaus cast him a very wicked look, but he didn't say anything.

'I think,' continued Roland. 'I think I know something about you. Something more than your wickedness which I don't doubt. I don't doubt it at all and it has my respect, being pure and in the blood. But I know something that is there too, in the blood as you say. Something you can't resist, something, apart from wickedness, Stanislaus can't resist.'

'What are you talking about?' whispered Stanislaus turning just a little pale. 'There is nothing, nothing in the world Stanislaus can't resist, except wickedness. Why that is how I got my name.'

'And what about gambling? What about a game of cards, Stanislaus? A wicked game of cards? I know what's in your pocket. I know that Stanislaus the Wicked always carries a pack of cards because it's something, he cannot resist. It's *in the blood*. Why you might as well have been given the name of *Stanislaus the Gambler*. And I even think some people have called you that.'

'Only on a night so dark that I can't see them,' said Stanislaus. 'Well, you are the first one who has called me that, to my face. And you are nothing, just a manky familiar. Why you are lucky, if you were anything *more* than a manky familiar, I would have your guts for garters, and I really mean it.'

No one spoke and Stanislaus looked uncomfortable, as if the silence was too much for him, too much for his wickedness.

'Well,' he said. 'If you weren't such a familiar, such a manky contemptible familiar, I wouldn't do it. But here goes. Here are the cards. You deal first.'

He put two decks of cards on the table. The duchess pointed to two of her daughters who got up so that they could both sit down.

'What are you playing?' she asked.

'Magic blackjack,' replied Stanislaus. 'We are playing magic blackjack. The queens count as tens, in honour of the duchess. Kings and jacks count as nine, tens and nines count as nine and eight, and so on. Ace of diamonds and clubs, take way one; ace of clubs counts as one, ace of hearts, take away nine, or less if you want, but always more than three. One of the queens is magic. She appears whenever she feels like it. She winks at you, so you can't mistake her.'

Roland dealt. The duchess took a couple of crabs and put one in each ear.

'What are you playing for?' she asked, trying to sound calm.

'The first game is just for fun. We play for crabs. We divide them equally between us. One pile each.' He heaped them up. The crabs looked miserable and moved their eyes this way and that, but he paid no attention. Roland dealt.

'Stop marching, you bloody wolards,' shouted Stanislaus. 'I need silence. I must have all the silence in the world. This is life.'·

The wolards lifted their feet up and down but in complete silence. Everything seemed to have stopped. Even the crabs didn't move. The only moving thing was the wave of marching feet, up and down, up and down but not making a sound. It was like an army of ghosts.

'Well…' whispered the duchess.

'Twenty-one,' said Stanislaus. 'Give me a crab.'

The Wask was standing behind Roland. Now he knew quite a bit about magic blackjack and the way Roland was playing didn't feel good. He seemed to have lost his

concentration and his pile of crabs was getting smaller and smaller. He was staring at his hand, but when it came to playing, he would throw down a card in a wild way and look surprised at the result.

'I am bust,' he said finally. 'I am bust, Stanislaus.'

'Give me your crabs,' said Stanislaus. 'And now you have tried what it is like to play *Stanislaus the Wicked, Stanislaus the Gambler.*'

'One more game, Stanislaus,' whispered Roland in a whisper the Wask only knew too well. The whisper of the gambler who has lost everything and wants to lose even more. It's a crazy thing is gambling and it is in the blood alright, even more perhaps than wickedness. There was Stanislaus and there was Roland, two gamblers sitting opposite each other. God help them.

'What for?' asked Stanislaus. 'What are we betting? What are the stakes?'

'The duchess and the duchy.'

'They are mine. What have you got?'

'A telescope and a bag. The telescope belonged to the Wask's grandfather and great-grandfather, and great-great-grandfather and perhaps even further back then that. It is a fine telescope. You can see everything in the world, all you have to do is wish.'

'That sounds like a wonderful thing. Let me try it.' The Wask sighed and gave it to him. 'I want to see the wicked witch, the Queen of the Witches asleep in her bedroom. Yes, there she is. What a telescope!'

'It's all I have got,' whispered the Wask. 'And it makes me who I am.'

'Stop moaning,' said Stanislaus 'Stop moaning and pull yourself together. Now what's in the bag?'

'Never mind that,' said Roland. 'It just happens to be my only possession. A manky bag for a manky familiar.'

'You can say that again. Well, I am dealing now.'

They kept playing till late into the night, moving their stakes around. Magic blackjack is a difficult game and complicated in every way. You can put in and withhold stakes, as well as refuse them. Roland seemed a bit steadier as the game wore on, but still he did more losing than winning. The duchess didn't say a word and the wolards kept up their silent march. Her sons and daughters gave Roland their jewels and their fancy buttons and soon he had lost them all. The pile of things in front of Stanislaus kept growing till all Roland had was the telescope and the bag.

'The duchess for the bag, that manky bag,' laughed Stanislaus feeling brave and wanting to throw a bit of caution to the wind. 'And now the number is eighteen. Neither of us must get more than eighteen. I am giving you a chance.'

They played. Roland put down a queen.

'Bad luck,' said Stanislaus. 'All the queens have gone and the nines count as eight.'

He turned his card and there it was: the queen of diamonds making twenty. He stared at it. The duchess winked. The card winked. It was a magic card and Stanislaus could not take his eyes off it. Sweat was dripping from his forehead and his hands were shaking. The queen of diamonds was looking at him and smiling wickedly. Stanislaus was staring at the card as if bewitched.

'Play for the duchy,' whispered the card in a strange high pitched voice. 'Now for the Duchy of Dronymore.' Again the queen winked. Then she became very still and flat looking, just like an ordinary card.

'For the Duchy of Dronymore,' said Roland, gathering the cards and dealing. Everyone was silent. Stanislaus sat there very stiff and pale as if he wasn't sure any longer where he was. Absentmindedly he took a crab and attached it to his nose. He glanced at his two cards and took another.

'I'm bust,' he whispered.

'Twenty-one,' said Roland. 'Twenty-one with the queen of diamonds. The magic card.'

He put down his cards. The queen winked, took off her crown and waived it like a hat. Again she winked, put the crown back on, opened her mouth as if to say something but remained silent. No one spoke. The queen winked and was still. The Wask kept looking at the card. The queen seemed to be changing shape, growing fatter. Yes, there was no mistaking it: she had turned into the duchess, only she was wearing a crown. The duchess grabbed the card and stuffed it in an enormous green handbag by her chair. She looked triumphant.

'Leave my duchy at once,' she shouted banging the table so that the crabs jumped into the air. 'Absolutely at once! You have lost, you monkey, you rapscallious knave, scoundrel, scallywag and contemptible loser—what are you waiting for? You can take your marching wolards and march them somewhere else, to the other side of the moon and beyond the Mountains of Fire and the Mountains of Ice where the dragons live and lay their eggs that hatch every thousand years. Go!'

Stanislaus stood up. He was very straight, very pale and his black eyes shone.

'Give me the bag,' he whispered. 'Or will you play for that?'

'It's yours,' said Roland pushing it across the table. The bag jumped up and down. The eye was furious but it couldn't do anything. You can't do anything about magic blackjack, losers are losers.

'Come my wolards,' whispered Stanislaus the Wicked clutching the bag in his hand.

'Come you wolards. Follow me. It's a long journey and we must make a start. Perhaps we should sing a song. I like a song myself and marching wolards are all singing wolards too. It's in your blood to march and to sing.'

You could almost feel sorry for him. The wolards followed him marching along as if nothing had happened because wolards do not understand. They are marching still. Yes, if you listen carefully you can probably hear them marching and singing their song. They never stop. They always follow Stanislaus. Stanislaus can't stop because of the bag. The bag follows him wherever he goes, because it is his, since he won it. Inside is the eye, the wicked eye of the Queen of the Witches and it is if she herself were there looking at him night and day. Can you hear them?'

Everyone in Maxim's All Night Diner was silent. Suddenly we could hear the stamp, stamp, stamp of wolards. We could even hear Stanislaus himself.

'Let me in, please let me in for just a moment or two. I haven't had any rest since I last saw the duchess of Dronymore. And I have travelled, have I have travelled! Why I have been east of the sun and west of the moon.

And always with that wretched eye staring at me. Let me just have a moment in good company listening to a story or two. Please let me a have a little rest in Maxim's All Night Diner. Have pity friends, witches, goblins and hobgoblins. Have pity.'

'No way!' Shouted a very fat lady who was sitting by the door. 'You are not letting him in while I have still got breath in my body. Pity! He doesn't even know the meaning of that word!'

'Why the duchess herself,' exclaimed Maxim. 'What an honour. What an honour for us all.'

'And not just me,' said the duchess. 'Look who else is here.'

We all turned round. There, next to her was the Wask, looking pleased and thoughtful and a little out of place, being more of a creature of the sea, but he had made himself at home and was resting one of his flippers on the table. On his shoulder was Roland standing as tall as he could. And in the shimmering light something gold glistened on his chest: the order of the *Golden Sock and Stars*.

I couldn't stop looking at the three of them, the duchess, the Wask and Roland.

'Good isn't it Annabel,' said Roland waving at me. 'Wouldn't you be proud to wear it?'

'I'm going to do better than that,' I shouted across the room. 'Far better. You see!'

'And now,' cried the little goblin who had told the story, 'We want a story from Maxim himself. You must all admit that that *was* a good story. A story with bells on. But now it's Maxim's turn and no one can tell a story like him.'

At this all the witches, goblins and hobgoblins shouted and stamped their feet, creating a din like nothing in the world and quite drowning the sound of the wolards as they marched by.

'Stop,' cried Maxim lifting one hand and there was a hush as if a great sea had suddenly been calmed. 'Silence everyone. Witches, goblins and all creatures of magic and darkness alike. Silence and the great Maxim will tell a story. It's a story of trolls and unicorns, and it's a wicked one all right, although it's called *Bring in the Clowns*. That makes it sound nice and sweet, though it's nothing of the kind. Not at all. But then there is no knowing with stories. It is as if they all have a life of their own. And that, Annabel,' he said suddenly turning to me. 'That is something you won't forget.'

I looked at him and nodded, though I wasn't really sure what he was talking about. Stories, a life of their own? I looked round the hall and I could see that all eyes were on Maxim, that hairy troll standing tall, like a dark tree, old and gnarled in some scary wood where things aren't what they seem.

'Is that what happens,' I whispered. 'Is that what

happens to stories down here among witches and trolls, that they have a life of their own?'

'You're brave,' said Maxim. 'It takes some guts to interrupt and ask a question. But that might not help you when you're deep into your own story. Yes, they do. Stories have a life of their own and you never know where they are going, and some are much wilder than others. You have been warned and you better remember that when you are telling *your* story. But now it's time for *Bring in the Clowns*.'

6

Bring in the Clowns

'ONCE UPON A time, a long time ago and before anyone had ever heard of Maxim's All Night Diner, trolls and witches lived quite apart. There was no singing and no dancing and no getting together for a good old talk or a story or two. No, every one minded their own business and the silence was awesome. There was plenty of magic about, but people didn't admire each other's magic, as they do now, nor did they show off. They kept themselves to themselves and they did their tricks when they felt like it. They were solitary folk and the only thing they cared about was magic itself, and at that they were far better than anyone before or since. Now something happened to change that world into this world of roaring sound and endless talk, and what happened is really surprising. I can't stop thinking about it, although I have probably seen more things than most people, having spent so much time with witches, hobgoblins and unicorns and other strange creatures. There are bits of the story, I still find puzzling and confusing because nothing is straightforward when there is magic, mystery and a fair amount of evil involved. No, you can never be sure, but I shall tell what I know and you can make your own minds up. It's not a story you want to tell too often. No, it's got quite a ring to it, perhaps awesome is the best word. It is an awesome story, but here at Maxim's we have listened to stories that could make your ears drop off without blinking an eye.

In those solitary days there was a troll, a really big hairy one like me. He owned nothing in the world but a carpet, the clothes he stood up in, a fig tree, a lemon tree and a rose bush and he lived in a cave. The carpet could be rolled up and he used to carry it under his arm taking it with him wherever he went. He loved his carpet. It was worn and ancient but of a wonderful design, full of birds and beasts which had been hurled together in a swirl of a pattern so that it looked like the Milky Way, except there were no stars, just birds and magnificent beasts, all dancing this way and that and keeping each other company. The troll lived at the very edge of the world where you get the Northern Lights and the snow can be quite mountainous and difficult to get through, if you are a wee thing, but that didn't bother the him one bit. He liked the cold outside, and he was warm inside because there was a fire in his cave. The fire was of a magical sort which he had stolen from a couple of mermaids who, sick of the sea, had gone to live in the woods to bring up their children and teach them the ways of the world which in those days didn't amount to much. Leaving the sea hadn't been as straightforward as they had hoped because of their tails and fins, but the troll attached wheels to them and they would dart across the snow as elegantly as before in the sea. He stole their fire because he was always stealing things. It came to him naturally and he couldn't do much about it, but the fire was good and it never went out.

You have to imagine the Northern Lights, endless woods, a few animals here and there: moose, squirrels, foxes and hares. Outside his cave, where it was always winter, he had a garden full of snow sculpture; inside, he had a fig tree, a lemon tree and a rose bush but nothing else, not a blade of grass. He didn't know his name and he wasn't sure he had any, but he was happy in his way, and time passed easily as it did in those days, but hasn't done since for reasons no one can quite understand but it may have something to do with fire in the blood and a certain wildness that's taken hold. However that may be, one day he rolled himself up in the carpet—something he'd never done before. Then he stood up with his huge hairy feet firmly planted in the snow. Since the carpet reached his chin, he must have looked a sight, but of that he was quite unaware. He stood there for a little while gazing at his ice sculpture and thinking no doubt of his garden inside, the two trees and his bush, his pride and joy, which he wasn't to see again for a very long time. And when he did he was utterly changed — a troll who had seen more than most of us here, and that is saying something. And what you know, you can't unknow—not even in stories. And this is where it all really begins.' Maxim paused and looked round the room.

'Ready?' he asked. Everyone nodded: witches, familiars, goblins and hobgoblins. I even caught sight of a unicorn or two. It is an awesome place is Maxim's All Night Diner and anyone who is anything in the world of magic is usually there.

'Ready Annabel? Because tonight's stories are in honour of you. The first human to visit this place ever. And whether you leave and how you leave…well, that's a business for later.'

I nodded. 'Get on with it Maxim.'

He continued in his big booming voice, 'What you know, you can't unknow. That's a fact and not one to be forgotten in a hurry. Some people don't like to hear about trolls and would prefer that they didn't exist, or that they were smaller and different, and altogether easier folk. But a good story has, as I said, a life of its own which you can't deny it however much you try. And what is wicked will out. Oh, yes there is no containing it. And you shall have it, straight as it happened. It's an awesome tale. I hope you are sitting comfortably.'

We were and quite comfortably enough, though a few wanted to reach out for a last minute snack of the kind that was there—nests of sea-weed with eyes and toes lurking in them and looking around. The eyes that is, the toes just seemed there for decoration and didn't do much moving about. Some kind of dessert, it must have been because we had reached that point in the evening when no one is really hungry but some can't resist temptation when it is there in front of them, and on roller skates too. The duchess was helping herself, pilling stuff up on her plate, as if she had all night to eat, when Maxim sounded the gong and everyone stopped: the waiters and waitresses, the cooks down below in the kitchen, the familiars and the witches, the goblins, hobgoblins and a few pirates that I hadn't noticed before. Mrs Rainbow, Patrick's mother, leant over and whispered in my ear and a very strange whisper it was. It was very quiet, so low that it seemed that she was moving her lips at all, but as the whisper came closer, it became louder, till it roared inside my ear.

'Be careful. Be careful you don't get trapped in *this story*. You really wouldn't want that to happen!' And the voice laughed and the laughter filled my head as if a huge shell were covering my ear and giving it a roar.

'What do you mean trapped?'

'Well sometimes people get trapped inside stories. Little girls and boys in particular, because they don't

know what's good for them. Or what's bad—very bad. And they get trapped inside a story and never get out. Not ever, because they don't know *how*. Do you know how?'

'No. Not really.'

'There you are! So you better not get trapped.' And she giggled and nudged the little witch sitting next to her, the one with the very long hair. Again Maxim sounded the gong and this time all were silent.

'So there he was, rolled up in the carpet like a sausage, hairy head above, hairy feet below, tail sticking out, what a sight! The carpet fitted him snugly and he looked down to gaze at its wonderful pattern but he found that it had quite disappeared. There was nothing but a strange darkness below, a ring of darkness and further down his hairy feet. He found the sight of them quite comforting and familiar but he didn't have long to look because a voice was bellowing at him. Yes, bellowing is the word because it had depth like something that is born out of great cavern of a place. The jaws and the lungs of whatever produced that must be enormous, and deep as a cave.

'Where are we going, Master?'

When he didn't answer, the voice repeated but a little timidly. 'Where are we going?'

And when there was no response, 'don't you want to go anywhere?' It sounded disappointed, but still the troll didn't answer because it was so long since anyone had spoken to him that he had forgotten what you do when people speak. He just listened. He liked the voice. It was deep and mellow, but the troll didn't know what to do. It's a funny thing, but if trolls don't hear speech for a long time, they clear forget what to do with it. The question and answer, the you say and I say, is something they don't know what to do with and, in this case, the troll was just a gawping idiot with a ring of darkness round his middle. The voice almost despaired.

'We *must* go somewhere,' continued the voice. 'That is what *must* happen because you are wearing me. We don't have to go *far*.' And the carpet sighed.

'Oh,' replied the troll. It's a funny thing hearing a voice. The fig tree and the lemon tree didn't have voices, and I have never tried speaking to the rose bush. But if we *must* go somewhere then I would like to see the *Great Ice Palace* of the trolls. A unicorn I once knew told me all about it and he swore that it exists.'

'Are you sure?' asked the carpet sadly.

'Quite sure.'

'The Great Ice Palace is at the end of the world, as far as I know, because no one has ever asked me to go further than that and the trolls who live there have a wickedness all of their own. A very special wickedness. It takes your breath away.'

'I am not frightened of anything,' said the troll. 'At least I don't think so. And it would be so wonderful to sail through the air swish, swash to the land of pure ice and snow.'

There was silence. The wind played with the endless snow and shook a few trees.

'You asked for it,' said the carpet finally. 'It's your wish, and I'm minding my own business, as I always do. I have learnt that nothing good comes of telling people what to do. So put your arms down and squeeze me really tight, as tight as tight can be. Hold on for dear life, we will be going faster than a leopard, flying through the air. You won't know yourself, not when you get that feel of pure speed— nothing but fastness and the roar of a thousand winds.'

The troll felt himself being lifted up. There was a roaring all around as the wind hit his face and brushed his hair back.

'I wonder what I look like from down below,' wondered the troll. 'Probably just like a black arrow with a tail and big ears. Lord, I feel as if my ears are being blown off. And the mountains down below! What mountains and streams, what a higgledy-piggledy of trees, as if those mountains hadn't shaved their cheeks. There is even a nice random sprinkling of bears moving like ants across that ridge. Bears know what they want, in the way of lonely folk who don't ask anyone else about their business, and mind their own. I feel quite like a bear myself, except I am a troll and there is nothing in the world like a troll—nothing at all—and at this moment nothing could be more wonderful than being just me: a flying troll going bang through the clouds at a speed that would knock out a leopard cold, make a panther wink and a unicorn hold on to his horn for dear life. Yes, being rolled up in this carpet and flying through the air is the most magnificent thing in the whole world and the best that has ever happened to anyone since time began.'

'Just wait,' sighed the carpet. 'Just wait.'

'I can't,' squeaked the troll out of breath with the roar of the wind. 'I can't.'

'That's what they all say, but you have things coming to you. One thing after another in the *Great Ice Palace* of that troll who has eyes like melons, feet the size of tables and hands like bicycles. He sits on a throne of green ice in the *Hall of a Thousand Echoes*. Well, I have warned you, but no one ever listens to me. No, as soon as someone has rolled himself up in me, he is overcome by a great longing to see the strangest and weirdest things he can think of, and danger means nothing, on the contrary, it's like a wicked perfume that has entered his brain and he's quite drunk on it. Well, we are getting closer. Are you ready?'

'Ready,' whispered the troll. 'Ready for the ice palace.'

'And the ice devils and the great troll himself?'

'Quite ready.'

'Well, that's what they all say. Suit yourself.'

And the troll found himself descending. It was the most beautiful feeling, a gentle floating on a breath of air. Suddenly everything became clear and he could see the *Great Ice Palace* below him: a mass of crazy spires, turrets and drawbridges. It was impossible to see any pattern and some of the paths and bridges seemed to lead nowhere. Here and there massive towers stood on lonely crags in awesome isolation. There were places, thought the troll, where you wouldn't want to be, and quite a few of them. He began counting them and then he stopped.

'One should never do anything too soon,' thought the troll. 'There is time for everything. But there is a pricking in my thumb—yes, there is evil here all right. Evil and badness and pure wickedness. There is a pricking in my thumb but what comes, must come.'

'We will start with the grandmother of the *Great Ice Troll*. That's the best I can do for you. She is almost the only non-wicked thing in the whole wicked place,' said the carpet in his deep mellow voice. 'She's lived here for hundreds of years and seen more things than even I dare think of, and I have been to strangest places. Well, once someone gets a magic carpet round their middle, there is no stopping them, no stopping them at all. But the time will come when you will miss those trees, lime and a fig wasn't it? And a rose bush, too.'

'There is always a time when you miss something, but I'm never going to regret anything. Never, ever,' replied the troll. 'And wickedness is something I can take in my stride.'

'Let's shake hands on that,' said the carpet unrolling itself and beginning to vanish into the air. 'But what is your name?'

The troll looked thoughtful.

'Easy,' he said at last. 'I think my name is Easy. My mother used to call me that all those years ago, before she left me with the unicorn. 'He's easy,' she would say, 'you just put him to sleep and Bob's your uncle. He's easy.' The unicorn didn't call me anything at all. He never really spoke.'

'Well, that's the weirdest thing I've ever heard,' whispered the carpet and vanished.

There, in front of him stood a big troll with ears hanging down to her shoulders, and a basket on her head.

'Well if that isn't a wee troll who must have got himself lost because no one ever comes here, unless they have to.'

She took the basket off her head.

'You're in luck,' she said. 'Plain lucky because I have got a basket full of cakes and there is no magic in them. None at all—and you'll be glad of that because no one likes the magic that's around here. It's so wicked, so very, very wicked that even I can't get used to it and I have been here more years than I can count, several hundred at least, or maybe even a thousand.'

'What's magic?' asked the troll.

'You must come from very far away—very, very far if you don't even know what magic is. In fact, you must be that wee troll who lived with a unicorn all on his own—a unicorn, two trees and rose bush and surrounded by great fields of snow. I am amazed that you can say anything at all.'

'So am I,' replied the troll. 'Words are a funny thing and I don't know what to do with them, but what did you say about cakes? And please, will you explain the word magic? By the way, my name is Easy.'

'Goodness, you are a natural talker; anyone can tell that. Now magic is a special *oomph*, which takes you by surprise and if you are around here, the surprise is usually unpleasant, messy, horrible and the worst you can imagine times seven and often it can't be undone. Well, let's face it, it can hardly ever be undone, no sirree. Whatever it is, you are stuck with it, and stuck may be the operative word: the bats' wings, pig's ears, you name it, you've got them and you might as well get used to them. My grandson is in charge of everything around here. He's the ice troll, and there's more wickedness packed into his heart than letters in a letter box, bananas in a crate or cakes in this basket. And here's one for the journey, a splendid doughnut just covered in sugar.'

'Any advice?' asked the troll shyly.

'Advice? Not, much. You need luck more than advice, far more. But I would say that you shouldn't speak, unless you're spoken to, and it's a good thing to keep your wits about you, if you've got any, but I doubt that. No there isn't much more I can say, but here's a key. Find the lock, and you're made. Don't find it and you're done for. And if you see my grandson, tell him Grandma sent you.'

She lifted the basket, put it on her head and walked straight on with her big ears swinging and her bottom moving from side to side.

So there he was, right smack in the middle of the ice castle on the very edge of the world and with as much common sense in him as you find in a puppy. He really didn't know anything. He'd spent his time with a silent unicorn, two trees and a rose bush and he thought his name was Easy. It's difficult to imagine a worse state of affairs, it really is. The world of magic needs so much more than common sense, and this fellow didn't even have *that*. He didn't have anything, except the clothes he stood up in and a key given him by an old lady of the troll race who might be as wicked and unreliable as anything. Can you trust a carpet, and a magic one at that? What can any one of us trust in this world?'

'Don't ask big questions,' said Mrs Rainbow. 'Just get on with your story.'

'Well, I just wanted you all to imagine what it must have felt like to be this troll who had just had the chill taken off his loneliness, only to find himself absolutely on his own in the middle of the biggest ice palace in the world. A crazy ice palace with random turrets and towers, paths all higgledy and piggledy and probably leading nowhere or to a somewhere you didn't want to go. He understood that there was danger around. Even he couldn't miss that.

Well, he brushed the snow off his furry head, gave his tail a shake and took a bite out of his doughnut. He'd never had a cake before and, in fact, no one knows what he'd been living off all those years. Probably berries and some kind of porridge made out of bark, the sort of things that unicorns eat because they've got too much soul to be fussy about food and basically don't care.

That bite made a difference: his teeth sank into some-thing they'd never felt before, a big soft something with a sugary crust.

'I am a real troll at last,' thought Easy. 'The world is mine. I can deal with any troll that comes my way. I am pretty big myself.' This is what a bite out of a doughnut made him feel. And there was no magic in that, no magic at all. He was just growing up, as we all have to do—creatures of the day and creatures of the night. Trolls and goblins, and witches too. Growing up casts a spell on all of us, and it isn't always easy, but it has its moments and standing there in front of the mightiest tower of all—well, that wasn't a moment he was ever going to forget. But he didn't have long to think about it because he happened to notice a gargoyle. Gargoyles are stone creatures that decorate ancient buildings. They are as dead as dead can be and a regular mishmash of eyes, noses and tails fixed onto bodies too old for words—well, this was an ice gargoyle, of course, and not dead at all. Its huge bulbous eyes seemed be staring at him and it had a wicked grin on its face. Its body was some kind of tail covered in scales so it looked like a snake with the face of an old man. The troll had seen it because it was just above the huge entrance set in a tower that greeted him like the jaws of some vast creature ready to swallow him up. But he didn't really notice it until it *rolled* its eyes. Then it stuck its tongue out and made a funny face.

'Hiya,' said the gargoyle and laughed. 'Well if that isn't a little troll.'

'Big,' replied Easy. 'A big troll.'

'Won't argue,' said the gargoyle. 'But you'll meet an awful lot of bigger trolls around here. Much, much bigger and then there is the Ice Troll himself. Now he's someone, quite someone. Oh, yes.'

'What do you mean?'

'Bigger. And I mean bigger. Hairier. Much hairier. And nastier. Altogether trollier. There is troll and there's more troll, and even more troll, and too much troll. You can definitely get too much troll. The ice troll is the trolliest troll there ever was. His hair is so thick you can hardly see his ears, though being troll ears they are even bigger than mine, and that's saying something.'

'You can't get enough troll.'

'You haven't tried. You must be that wee troll who lived all alone with a unicorn which must have given you a great longing for other trolls and trolliness. Well, you are going to get plenty of troll now. More than you bargained for.' And the gargoyle became silent and as still as the ice it was made of. Its big bulbous eyes seemed fixed on nothing at all.

'Please talk to me. I like anything that talks.'

But the gargoyle didn't say a word and his face was quite still. So Easy began to cross the drawbridge in front of the tower that stood as a giant entrance to the palace.

The closer he got, the more it resembled the jaws of some strange creature. He kept his eyes fixed on the gargoyle in case it said anything. He was just about to give up hope when it suddenly rolled its eyes again.

'Watch out for trolls,' whispered the gargoyle in a thin voice. 'Watch out for trolls and try to find the clowns. They'll make you laugh. And you'll need that. Boy, will you need that.'

'Clowns?' asked Easy who had never heard of clowns. 'Clowns?'

The gargoyle didn't reply.

'Well, I shall try to find them, whatever they are. I trust that fellow up there. I think he knows what he is talking about.' He wrapped the remains of his doughnut in a red handkerchief he always kept in his pocket. His mother had given it to him and that made it special. As he went through the tower, he could hear the gargoyle giggling and whispering to itself. 'Look at that wee troll on his voyage of discovery with nothing but a doughnut in his pocket and a magic key. He hasn't a thought in his head. Well, we won't be seeing him again, unless he finds the clowns, and they are well hidden. Well and truly hidden. Why, no one has seen them for years. Years and years.'

As he came through the entrance, the troll saw a vast square covered in ice and snow with a wall all around it. It was a very strange sight. It was as if a place full of life had been transformed into a silent ice world. He couldn't believe his eyes. There were huge fountains sprouting jets of ice into the air and trees with ice fruit and ice flowers. When he looked closely, he thought he could see animals, but made of ice, as if touched by a sudden arctic wind. Why, there was an ice fox about to pounce on a rabbit, and the strange thing was that the fox looked strong and sure of himself and the rabbit full of fear. A bear was preparing to catch a fish from a pond, his paw in the air. Everything was just about to happen, but nothing did. Nothing at all. The place was full of life and not full of life. The longer he looked, the more creatures he saw, and the more he could feel a strange silence creeping up on him. Slowly he turned round. Within the arched entrance of the tower stood a couple of ice crows with their beaks on the ground as if looking for food. He hadn't noticed them before and he thought they couldn't have been there, because they were smack in the middle of the path and he would have fallen over them on his way to where he was now. When he looked down, he saw that some ice mice were nibbling at his toes. New creatures kept appearing and the landscape changing, although the moment of change was always hidden. It was as if looking made things appear. He would have sworn that that tower with its crisp ice flag hadn't been there before. No, there had been nothing right in front of him. And the army of men some in front, some on the top of the tower. He was certain that they hadn't been there before.

'Just look for the clowns,' he heard the calm voice of the gargoyle coming now from far away. 'Just look for the clowns. Go straight ahead, turn left by the armadillo. You can't miss him. He's got a fat belt around his middle and a long tail. He looks like nothing else in the world and is really pleased with himself. Follow the path till you come to a door. Knock on it. If it likes you, it will open without any fuss. Tell the first creature you meet that I sent you. Say you bring greetings from the gargoyle of the West Tower. I'm quite famous in these parts you know. And remember you are not mad or going mad. This place *is* mad. It's one of the maddest places in the world, but you are a troll and trolls can deal with madness. Good luck, Easy. Remember me. Remember the gargoyle of the West Tower and find those clowns.'

He found the armadillo immediately and the door too. It was so tiny he had to creep in on all fours and when he stood up, he found himself in a low corridor lit by candles that were standing in niches in the wall. There weren't many of them and the place was full of shadows and darkness. A huge cage hung down from the ceiling. In it was an enormous bird with long tail feathers. Unlike everything else, it was alive and moving. What a relief! The troll sighed.

'Greetings from the gargoyle of the West Tower. Would you like a bit of my doughnut?'

'Goodness it's a troll. A wee troll.'

'I am big, a very big troll, but everyone here calls me a wee troll.'

'That's just because we are used to the big Ice Troll. The biggest troll there ever was. He's as big as a house. Wait till you see him.'

'I'm not sure I want to. '

'Beggars aren't choosers. You'll see him whether you want to or not—and he'll see you. Where's the dough-nut?'

Easy broke off a piece of his doughnut and the bird ate it.

'His granny made that, I am sure. She's the only one who makes cakes around here. Now for your question and don't tell me you've forgotten it. Everyone who comes asks me a question. Completely useless questions. Silly, billy questions but I always answer because I'm a polite bird, the only polite thing in this whole blasted, crazy place. So tell me your question and I'll try my best.'

'Where are the clowns?' asked Easy wondering what clowns were. 'Where are the clowns?'

'Now that's a question, a real question. I have been waiting for that. Waiting for a thousand years or what feels like a thousand years. Where are the clowns indeed! They are deep down under ground, beneath all this ice, beneath all these ice towers, turrets, drawbridges, moats and what not. Beneath the great hall of the Ice Troll who has made all of this. Deep down below are the clowns and the whole circus; a great big circus tent, and the caravans they came in. It's all there but it's gone to sleep and covered in cobwebs. Dust and cobwebs. That's all there is where there were red noses and laughter. God knows what made them come here, but they did. One day a circus arrived with jugglers and tigers and clowns and tightrope walkers. The whole kit and caboodle, as they say, and all dressed up too. What fancy costumes, and not just the jugglers and the tight ropewalkers. Oh, no. The horses had feathers and the tigers chains round their necks and the elephants wore hats. Well, I think they were elephants because I am not used to that kind of animal, being from around here, the kingdom of ice and snow. They had long noses which they kept on the ground and the ice king's daughter thought they were anteaters and said elephants were bigger, but she wasn't sure. But that doesn't matter, because they are all deep down below now and no one has seen them for years and years and most of us have forgotten what laughter is. I keep reminding myself by laughing once a week. Once a week I jump up and down making a deep rumbling sound in my throat and I keep going till it sounds about right. No sooner is the sound there, that beautiful sound, then the Ice Troll shouts, 'Silence. Silence, you stupid bird or I'll wring your neck!' My, what a temper he has.'

The bird stopped talking. It seemed upset. It had huge,

sad eyes and was looking at the bottom of the cage as if it had lost all hope. Its wings were tightly folded onto its chest and its shoulders were hunched.

'Have you got a golden key?' it asked suddenly. 'Because if you have then you can open my cage and I'll squeeze myself into a ball and sit in your pocket. I swear, I'll be useful—I'm the only useful thing around here and I have saved the lives of ever so many creatures. Even pirates, though we don't get many of them being so far from the sea. No, I'm a well-respected and glorious bird. Glorious is the word and it's not my fault that the wicked Ice Troll has put me in a cage. I don't belong here at all, but he is so wicked he doesn't care and it's no good talking to him. But you—you need a glorious bird in that pocket of yours. Why it's crying out for one.'

The troll looked down at his pocket and he could see that the bird would fit snugly inside and he felt that there was nothing he wanted more than that bird with all its talking and fiery temper. So he opened the cage and the bird jumped into his pocket.

'Now get going,' shouted the bird. 'There isn't a moment to lose.'

'But where? '

'Why straight ahead. You can't go any other way, unless you want to go back and I really wouldn't advise *that*.'

Ahead meant a stone passage with doors firmly shut

and only pale beams of light leading into nothing but darkness.

'What happens at the end of the passage?' asked the troll.

'Don't ask that,' replied the bird. 'Don't or you'll just stay here.' And the bird giggled. 'Actually, I'm not quite sure. It's such a long time since I've been out of that blasted cage. Let's just hope it's not too horrible.'

The doors all had knockers but no handles. The knockers were yellow and shiny and each one was a different . Many of them had been made to look like animals: bears, tigers, lions, elephants, deer, giraffe and strange creatures who looked like they were a mixture of many things at once. On one door he saw the head of a troll.

'Let's not touch that one,' whispered the bird. 'That takes you to the office of the Ice Troll where he sits behind an enormous desk that he likes to bang with fists the size of melons. We want to find the clowns.'

When the troll looked closely at the knockers, he could see that they were moving. The lions and tigers were roaring and the elephants were waving their trunks. He didn't know that they were elephants of course and the bird wasn't sure what they were and didn't seem to care. The walls were covered in ice and this made them look shiny and black. Here and there a lamp hung down from the ceiling with a timid and ghostly light. It was an awesome place and he would probably have been frightened if the bird had stopped talking, but it never did. It went on and on, about this and that. The Ice Troll was the wickedest thing in the world and so jealous he couldn't tolerate another living creature near him that had any gumption at all, and so he sat on a throne all day in the great ice palace and sulked. He could sulk the tail off a skunk and the trunk off an elephant. He hated clowns more than anything in the world, for no reason at all, except once he had begun hating something he couldn't let go and his hatred wormed itself into his heart, till there was nothing left of him except the things he hated. He had a long list of the things, he hated most and he had it read out every morning to the blast of a trumpet. He would sit there in the *Great Hall of a Thousand Echoes* on a throne of green ice while a young troll in tails—he liked everyone to be dressed up—read out the list of what he hated most. Two small trolls would take it in turn to blow a trumpet as each thing was read out. A special crowd invited to listen had to clap whenever the Ice Troll winked or rang a bell that stood on table next to his throne. This would go on for hours but no one dared stop. If you drew breath or failed to clap or smiled or did anything that he didn't like, the Ice Troll had you turned into ice and put in one of the parks that lay below the towers of his great ice castle. Why he did this was a mystery and something the bird couldn't understand at all. But it was a fact.

'And nobody has been able to do nothing about it for a thousand years or so,' said the bird. 'One day this circus arrived out of the blue. The performers knew nothing about the Ice Troll. They were just lost. They put up their big top and invited the Ice Troll to come and watch a performance. They gave him a special seat because he's as big as a horse. He was watching all right for a little while, although he did seem a bit confused and taken by surprise. And weren't we all? Why no one here had ever seen anything like it. The warmth of it, the smell of the animals, the noise and the to do, and the costumes! The Ice Troll loves dressing up, as I've told you—but that was nothing. Nothing compared to this: the wigs and the noses, the shoes and the taffeta, the lights and the sparkle, and the colours of their faces! The clowns were the best of all. Those big red mouths, white cheeks and big black eyebrows. And what eyes! The trolls were all agog: little trolls, and big trolls, all sitting together as close as close because there wasn't that much room in the big top, once everyone had a seat. There were lots of trolls in the castle then—the place was a riot of trolls, but they've all been banished now.'

'Where are they?' asked Easy.

'They're in the big top. Sitting as they sat, their big troll eyes fixed on the performance that doesn't take place, on the clowns who don't move, listening to the orchestra which doesn't play. All as it was that moment, when the Ice Troll raised his hand and asked it all to stop. Just like that. The clowns were standing in the middle of the ring and all the trolls were stamping their feet. The din was tremendous. The Ice Troll was sitting quietly in his place as if nothing bothered him at all, but you never know what he is thinking, what is taking place behind that brow. Then one of the clowns asked for someone to come into the ring and help them with something. You had to stand on top of a barrel and hold something and all the trolls wanted to do it and they were all yelling.

'I won't do anything, unless you are all quiet,' said the clown. 'All completely silent. I want it to be so quiet that I can hear the pitter patter of the feet of a mouse running across the sawdust in the ring.' He took a mouse out of his pocket and let it go.

'Pitter, patter,' whispered the clown looking very stern with his great big eyebrows. The trolls were all silent. The clown was looking at each row as, if he had all the time in the world. But he didn't pick any of the ordinary trolls. No, suddenly he pointed at the Ice Troll himself—the great Ice Troll! I don't think he knew anything about trolls—he certainly didn't know the Ice Troll, or he wouldn't have done it.

'Come into the ring,' said the clown.

The Ice Troll got up, the trolls began to stamp their feet but then they all froze as he raised his hand and said stop. That was it. He raised his hand and looked round as if he were the king of the world, which he is in his way. He's certainly the king of all that's here in the Kingdom of Ice.

'Stop,' he said. The clowns looked as if they were about to speak but then the sheer magic of his big troll face made them silent and still and that silence and stillness spread like a wave across the rows of trolls. And they are still sitting, as they sat. They're all in the big top, deep down below.'

Easy looked down the long hall in front of him. The dark stones were shiny and wet and there seemed to be no end to this hall of shut doors and strange knockers. He kept wondering how deep down he was. He could tell he was going down because of the angle of the shafts of light which were further and further apart. The bird kept talking. It seemed to know almost everything. It was called Miranda and was a bird of many colours, probably a parrot. That was one of the few things, it wasn't quite sure about.

'But I've got wonderful plumage. That's a special word for feathers. My plumage is magnificent. Out of this world. And the next.'

'Do you know anything,' asked Easy timidly. 'Anything about trolls?'

'Not a lot—but that's because there isn't so much to know. I've lived my life among trolls. I was a present from the Queen of the Witches to the great Ice Troll and I arrived in a golden cage carried by four little witches. Everyone kept looking at my feathers—they had never seen such a bird in the Kingdom of Ice. Such plumage. I had never seen a troll before and I had never seen anything hairier. Trolls are very proud, but you have to be careful what you say to them. Things march slowly through their heads, one at time and you don't want to hurt their feelings. They like company, although they argue a lot and have fierce tempers. Why, you are the first solitary troll, I've ever met.'

'That's an accident,' said Easy.

He had never heard such talking and he discovered the strangest things about trolls and their history.

'I never lie,' said the bird. 'Not completely and utterly, but sometimes I get lost in my own stories and have to invent bits and pieces to do the joinings together and make my stories whole. Nothing makes sense, if you just stick to what you know. Anyhow, you're a funny fellow and I'll have to tell you that I have never met anyone less street wise. Why you don't know your own hairy feet from a leprechaun!'

The troll didn't say a word. He just listened. He never wanted to part with that bird. It had a way with talking. Suddenly the hall came to end and there was just a door. A small non- descript door which was so unexpected that the troll walked straight into it. The door opened. There they were, in the big top.

In the big top with the clowns and the trolls and the orchestra and the animals. But it was all dead silent and the place was so full of darkness, you couldn't really make out anything till you were almost right on top of it. The dust and the cobwebs were something incredible. They covered everything, as if scattered by a giant's hand. The troll looked up, expecting a giant there because the whole thing seemed somehow controlled and arranged. But the silence convinced him that it wasn't so—the dust and the debris had just grown around everything like snow covering a landscape. Time was well settled here and didn't move. The clowns stared and the audience stared back, but one couldn't tell whether there was any sight in those eyes and the lack of movement was enough to drive you crazy and yet seemed catching, as if you might any moment become part of the spell. The troll stood in the door, wanting neither to leave or stay, and at the same time terrified that he might become part of this strange landscape. He noticed that the floor was full of mice and beetles and other scampering creatures whose tiny movements made an exaggerated noise. The more he looked, the more he could see. A spider was chasing a beetle down the cheeks of the nearest clown who had been caught in the middle of making a forceful movement with a trumpet that he held in his outstretched hand. He had one enormous shoe in front of the other. Perhaps he was the one who had invited the Ice Troll to come into the ring and join the performance. He looked determined. The beetle swung himself from the clown's chin onto his trousers, the spider followed, his thread dangling behind.

'So this is a circus,' whispered Easy. 'And that is what clowns look like. I was wondering what you were talking about. I am a troll who doesn't know much about the world.'

'Yes, this is it. We're in the big top. I am sorry this is your first time in a circus tent —and this was a beauty. Red and white stripes—but you can hardly tell that now.'

'It looks like folds of a brown and grey something.' The troll touched the side of the tent and his big nails went straight through it and there was a huge tear. He picked up a stool that was just inside the ring and the leg came off in his hand. He let it fall and it broke into many pieces. The bird flew out of his pocket and made a circle of the tent. He watched it flying round and round, a splendid thing of colour and movement making the place seem all the more ghostly and creepy. There was no life in these clowns, no life in the trolls and he thought they had no business sitting there, looking at one another. It was magic but of an awesome and maddening kind. Suddenly the door behind them burst open and there he was, the great Ice Troll himself.

'What are you doing here?'

Easy didn't say a word. He could feel himself becoming as cold as ice, and he knew that when all of him felt like ice, then he would become just like the clowns and the trolls, a thing sitting or a thing standing and just something for mice and beetles to play on.

'What are you doing here?' asked the Ice Troll in a voice so threatening that it didn't sound like a question at all. Now, you have to remember that Easy wasn't used to talking and so he would listen much too carefully to what people said.

'Watching the clowns,' replied Easy. 'That's what I am doing. I am watching the clowns. And I am eating a doughnut.' He took the rest of the doughnut out of his pocket and chewed on it thoughtfully. The Ice Troll closed the door behind him.

'I bring greetings from the gargoyle of the West Tower and your granny. She's the one who gave me this doughnut. The first doughnut I have ever tasted. And I have got a key, a golden key. A key and a bird. That bird there.' And he pointed at Miranda.

The Ice Troll listened because he hadn't expected all that information—not that he was interested—not at all, but he had never seen a troll like this one, and he wasn't really used to being talked to.

'I used to live all alone. All alone with a lemon tree and a fig tree, till I rolled myself up in a magic carpet and went whoosh through the air. That's how I came here and this is my first visit to a big top.'

'You won't be disappointed,' said the Ice Troll. 'I wasn't. It is the most horrible thing in the whole world— perfectly disgusting. Just look round you. Just look at those clowns. Well, I soon put a stop to that. '

'A stop to what?'

'The clowns. I put a stop to the clowns. No more clowning about. Just silence.'

'I know silence,' said Easy, 'I've been with silence ever since the unicorn left me. He walked out one day and never came back. The first thing I spoke to after that was your granny and a gargoyle. The gargoyle told me to look for the clowns. And here I am and I have found them.'

'You have found a lot more than that,' said the Ice Troll. 'A lot more.'

He sat down in the middle of the ring, just behind one of the clowns, as there happened to be a chair there. A huge thing like a throne, but you could see that some small rodent had been nibbling at it and it nearly collapsed under him.

'I think you're the only troll in the word who hasn't heard of me, the great Ice Troll. I am called that because I live in a great palace of ice and I think ice thoughts and I have ice blood. They say even my heart is made of ice. Whatever entered the heads of those clowns? The circus was well and truly lost and now it's got what is deserved and had coming to it.'

Miranda was perched on a trapeze that hung down from the centre of the big top.

'You shouldn't have let out that bird. It belongs in a cage,' said the great Ice Troll. 'Everything belongs in cages. Freedom is a bad thing, particularly for birds.'

The Ice Troll looked up at Miranda. A feather fell slowly, landing on the shoe of a clown who was standing in the middle of the ring looking up. Easy continued to eat his doughnut. He didn't really understand. You have to imagine someone who is really clueless, who really couldn't tell his own hairy feet from a leprechaun, who wasn't streetwise at all, who had no notion of the strange possibilities lurking inside others. This guy meant no harm and he only knew himself, and there wasn't much to know. He was a simple troll who'd got himself rolled up in a magic carpet by pure accident having spent years with two trees, a rosebush and a unicorn who hardly spoke.

'What's your name?' asked the Ice Troll.

'Easy.'

'The only troll I've ever seen who reminds me of you was a crazy one who came wandering over the fields of snow years ago. She said her name was Complicated. I didn't know what to do with her. So I made her my cook and she's in charge of the huge kitchen, the only hot place in the Ice Palace. And, boy, is that place hot. It glows.'

'That's my sister. There were two of us. Complicated and Easy. My mother used to say, 'He sleeps all night, he's easy. She screams all night, she's complicated. But they both get on my nerves.' She left one night and Complicated must have followed her across the plains and fields and mountains and got really lost.'

'No one comes here unless they are lost,' said the Ice Troll. 'Or stupid enough to roll themselves up inside a magic carpet.'

'Well here I am,' said Easy. 'And I have discovered that I like clowns and I like birds, particularly if they talk.' He looked round the big top: it was a creepy place, and, when no one spoke, the dead and alive clowns and trolls really made their presence felt. Here was one with his hands in a bag, probably just about to take out a sweet, and another with his face cupped in his hands waiting for the clowns to begin their act. The Ice Troll had taken a moment and fixed it. It was a piece of diabolical magic. And Easy just stood there eating his doughnut looking round at all those dead and alive creatures. He looked very thoughtful, but I don't think there was a thought in his head.

'What are you?' he asked quietly.

'That's a funny question, but I like it. I am evil, pure evil. I am the great Ice Troll and, yes, I have an ice heart. Easy, Complicated and Evil, what a get together.'

'What's evil?'

'Oh, all kinds of nastiness and smelliness and badness and wickedness, all rolled into one. I am really, really wicked. So wicked it takes your breath away and knocks you out. Knocks you out cold. There are many kinds of trolls in the world, but most of them fall into three kinds: the good, the bad and the ugly and variations of these like very good, very bad and very ugly. But I am a troll apart, because I am evil. Pure evil. And there is no messing with me.' The Ice Troll laughed and his laughter filled the big top and sent an echo round it.

'I am feeling very wicked and I have got a pricking in my thumb.'

Easy didn't say a word.

'My, you are calm. You really are easy. Easy come, easy go and calm as a cucumber.'

'What's a cucumber?' asked Easy.

'A funny sort of thing and very green. Don't like it much, but I like that way you are calm. That's the only problem with being evil, really evil. When you are as evil as I am, people can drive you just mad because they can't keep calm or still, unless you do a bit of magic. Just look at those clowns and those trolls. They've been sitting like this for years with only rats and mice for company. Now come with me.'

The Ice Troll got out of his chair and walked slowly towards the door. Easy and the bird followed. They walked down corridors with shut doors and they didn't see a soul. Finally, they came to the great hall itself. A small troll was standing beside the throne of the Ice Troll with a pencil and paper, ready to continue the list of all the things he hated. Two trolls were ready with their trumpets.

'Just look at him,' said the Ice Troll pointing. 'He's shaking already and I haven't even sat down on the throne. I haven't even sat down and I haven't even spoken to him. Now how far did we get?'

'Cattttt-tttter,' whispered the troll and dropped his pencil.

'Cater what?' boomed the Great Ice Troll. 'Cater-what?'

'Cattt-er, cater,'

'Speak slowly.'

'Cater, cater, caterpillars.'

'Caterpillars, of course. Why didn't you say that in the first place? I hate caterpillars. I have always hated caterpillars. I hated caterpillars before I had even ever seen one, but I particularly hated them after someone dropped one in my soup. Come on trumpets. Why, this is enough to drive one mad. Maybe you can do it, Easy. You take over reading.'

'Can't read,' said Easy. 'The unicorn never taught me. Don't know what reading is.'

'Can't read! Here I am, the most evil troll in the world and surrounded by fools and idiots. Can't even read— most witches can read and those who can't, pretend they can. Hobgoblins can all read. What's wrong with you? And why were you brought up by a unicorn?'

'Don't know,' said Easy. 'But I know what you could do. I know something you could do because you're evil —something to make that troll calm enough to read with someone so evil sitting next to him.'

'And what's that? I've tried everything—everything I can think of.'

'You could bring in the clowns,' whispered Easy.

'Bring in the clowns!'

'It wouldn't make you any less evil.'

'That depends.'

'Depends on what?' asked Easy and the great Ice Troll couldn't think of an answer and went all quiet. Or maybe a sudden longing for clowns came over him. There is no knowing with trolls, even the great Ice Troll. They are moody creatures, too moody perhaps for pure evil. No one said a word.

'Bring in the clowns,' boomed the voice of the great Ice Troll suddenly. 'Bring in the clowns,' echoed the walls of the Great Hall and the sound of the Ice Troll's voice travelled all through the palace till it reached the big top itself. And as soon as that happened, there they were, there in the Great Hall, their clothes still covered in dust and beetles in their hair. They didn't move for quite a few moments, as if getting used to the place. Then they looked at the troll with the pen and paper and one of the clowns smiled. It wasn't much of a smile: just a timid thing that spread slowly across his face, as if he didn't quite know what to do with it, and that isn't surprising really.

'Now read on,' cried the great Ice Troll. 'Read on. Read on as if your life depended on it.'

The little troll looked down at his paper and at his big hairy finger just below the next word. Then he looked up at the clown. He saw that the smile had definitely settled on his face and it seemed to be there for good. In his eyes he could see something else which might just be the beginning of laughter.

'Mice,' he said. 'You hate mice. The great Ice Troll hates mice.' He spoke quickly because he wanted to continue talking to the clown with his face and his eyes. The clown nodded and his eyes were saying, 'The great Ice Troll is a fool. A fool and an idiot.' And his smile said, 'Who cares about Ice Trolls?'

'Mice,' shouted the great Ice Troll. 'Do I hate mice! Sound trumpets sound. The great Ice Troll hates mice. Stop smiling, you silly clown!'

The eyes of the clown became big and sad, but the smile was still there. Then slowly, as if unwilling, it began to disappear till just a big round mouth was left. It was the funniest thing the little troll had ever seen, but he didn't laugh. The other clown put his hand in his pocket and took it out slowly. In it was a mouse.

'I am outraged!' shouted the Ice Troll, 'No one, but no one has ever done something like this in the Great Ice Hall. I will not have it. I shall stamp and stamp.' And he stamped and he let his huge fist hit the throne. Bits of wood and ice flew everywhere.

'I'll bang and I'll stamp,' shouted the Ice Troll. 'I shall do so, as if there were no tomorrow and till the cows come home. No one treats the great Ice Troll like this and gets away with it.' He hurled bits of his throne all over and his big hairy feet hit the floor like thunder. But in the rumpus and confusion everyone ran out of the door. The troll who had been reading and the trolls who had been playing the trumpet, the clowns and the bird and Easy. Everyone escaped, even the Ice Troll's grand-mother and the cooks in his kitchen. So when he stopped stamping, there was nothing but silence. And he's been moving in that silence ever since, in and out of turrets and towers and down those dark tunnels. Wherever he goes, empty echoes follow him, 'I am the great Ice Troll,' he shouts and from all around him the echoes fall, 'Ice Troll, Ice Troll.'

'But what happened to Easy?'

'Easy took another name. You can't be called Easy. The bird Miranda thought he should take the same name as the clown, the one who smiled. And Miranda has been with him ever since. And there she is.'

We all looked up to the rafters in the ceiling.

'What plumage!' said Mrs Rainbow.

'A fine bird,' said the Wask.

'And what was the name of the clown?' asked the little witch with red hair. 'The one who smiled?'

'What?' shouted Maxim. 'Am I surrounded by fools and idiots like the great Ice Troll?'

'Not entirely,' whispered Roland standing as tall as he could. 'Not entirely Maxim. Some of us have our wits about us and can understand a good story. So what happened to Complicated? She's your sister isn't she?'

'She certainly is and she runs another place like this. Like me she can't stop talking. She chatters like a bird. Hers is a fine diner, good food and good company in glorious surroundings, bats, chandeliers, the lot—but it's a long way from here. And all of that happened many years ago and the world is quite a different place now. Now there is no end of talking, as if to make up for all that time, and you have to look around for silence. Unless you happen to be the great Ice Troll, then you've got plenty of it.' He shook his head. 'Yes, he is among the turrets and the towers. He's quite lost his mind and it's all the same to him. 'Ice Troll, Ice Troll,' he shouts and the echoes return his cry. Sometimes he will run so fast, he bangs himself against the ice walls because he's always hoping that he's heard a voice other than his own. 'Can one die of loneliness?' he asks. What a question, and that from someone who thinks ice thoughts! And now for the last story. It's Annabel's turn. And be careful, or the hobgoblins will get you!'

All around there is a silence, but suddenly I'm no longer afraid. Yes, I'm prepared.

'Remember the hobgoblins,' whispers Mrs Rainbow.

'I haven't forgotten.'

'And don't get trapped. Don't get trapped in the story.'

'It's the worst that can happen to anyone, ever,' whispers the witch with long red hair.

'Leave her alone,' says Sinbad. 'Just leave her alone to do her own journey and take her own twists and turns in that story that's waiting for her, just waiting to swallow her up as stories do.'

'Are you ready?' shouts Maxim. 'You better be because I've waited long enough!'

I stand up so that everyone can see me and I can feel their eyes on me. Trolls, witches, goblins, hobgoblins and all the creatures of the night sitting here in Maxim's Diner are facing me. Slowly I step onto a chair and from there onto a table so that they can all see me. Stories, I'll give you stories...

There are no dragons in New York
or
Who's taken my hat?

I HAVE BEEN ASKED to tell a story and this is what I've been waiting for, waiting all night. Of course, I'm all pins and needles and wondering what to do. Yes, the hobgoblins might get me all right, no doubt about that because I've no secret stories up my sleeve, and yet … and yet…there is something, something lurking in my thoughts, something waiting to be told, to be unfurled and let lose upon this sea of listeners. If only I knew where to begin…

I look up to where Miranda is perched on the arm of a chandelier, but that bird has nothing to say to me. She was all talk, talk but now she's tickling her feathers, making herself beautiful. What a vain bird! Or perhaps she knows a hopeless case when she sees one and doesn't want to be caught paying too much attention when the hobgoblins come. Perhaps I'm a loser. I'm certainly on my own now. You don't have to tell me that, silly bird! I'll give you plumage!

The little witch with the red hair is laughing at me and what laughter! It's a laughter that dances round the room, bends and buckles moving like a snake. Yes, they are all laughing now. Goblins, hobgoblins, familiars and Maxim too, that hairy troll. He has picked up his tail and is looking at it, as if he's wondering what to do with such a thing, such a long hairy thing.

'Be careful,' he says. 'Take care or the hobgoblins will get you. We are very particular about stories here, aren't we?' Everyone nods, but in an off hand way, because they are all doing something with their feet or their hands or their eyes. Reaching out for some food or drink or looking round. No one is sitting still. I can tell that they are not expecting much, not of *me*. Well, I'm going to give them something to think about.

'Remember there must be sixteen Annabels in the story,' whispers Mrs Rainbow.

'Or the hobgoblins will get you,' adds Maxim wickedly. 'Watch out for those hobgoblins. They won't watch out for you.'

'What are you talking about?' asks Mrs Rainbow. 'The hobgoblins are always watching out, always on the look-out for a bad story teller.'

'So what is your story called?' asks a voice.

'Yes, what is it called?' Other voices, lazy, uninterested.

'Bet this one will be a slow one.'

'A silly one.'

'The hobgoblins will get her.'

'Silence,' shouts Maxim. 'Give her a chance!'

But still they continue talking. He lifts his arms into the air and fills his lungs, but even before he speaks there is silence. So he looks round, lets his arms fall and smiles.

'Now, what is it called? What's the name of your story?'

I learn its name, as I'm saying it, as the others are hearing it, because I have entered the story. I have become part of it.

'It's called, *'There are no Dragons in New York* or *Who's Stolen my Hat?'*

There is a silence all around me and I can feel myself getting right inside the story. It feels good and friendly —but you can't trust stories. It's got a strange name, a name that makes no sense, or no sense at the moment. There are no dragons in New York, and I have never worn or owned a hat, not as far as I can remember.

Maxim looks thoughtful. 'I have only been to New York once. It's not the kind of place where you would think of finding someone like me, yet there are one or two trolls there and quite few witches. At least there were when I was there, many years ago. I stayed inside the Statue of Liberty one night, after everyone had gone. There was only me and a goblin and we made the time pass by telling stories. Anyone else been to New York?'

'I've been to Grand Central Station,' says the duchess. 'Wonderful place that. I would really recommend it.'

And just as she says that I know that's where I am. I am on Grand Central Station and I can hear the voice of the duchess but it seems to be coming from very far away. I can hear other voices, and I know that back in Maxim's All Night Diner they're busy talking about New York and who has been there and who hasn't. It's one of those conversations that don't go anywhere, but that everyone enjoys because they've got something to say, and it's quite safe because there is a mellow mood about the place.

'It all began,' I hear myself saying. 'It all began on Grand Central Station. No, I mean, it all begins here, on Grand Central Station. Right here, right now, underneath this clock. I am waiting and I know who I am waiting for.'

'Do you?' asks the duchess.

'Are you sure?' asks Maxim.

'You never know who you will meet,' says Mrs Rainbow. 'Not in stories. Stories take you by surprise. That's what they are there for. Don't think *you* know everything, young lady.'

She's quite right of course. I'm waiting, but I don't know who I am waiting for. I have a feeling that I don't know anything at all and that *anything* could happen. But I do know that I am here for a reason. Yes, I am meant to be here, by this clock that shows half past three. Wait, the hands are now moving and they are moving pretty fast, round and round. Never have the hours passed so quickly. The clock has four faces. On two of them, I can see the hands moving. When they stop, it says four o'clock. That seems strange, all that round and round just to get to four. So it must be the next day or four at night. Now the four faces are showing different times.

'I have been waiting for you,' says a small man below a sign which says timetables. 'I have been waiting ever such a long time—since last Tuesday or Friday and I haven't been complaining or moaning or groaning. It's not the sort of thing I would do. And certainly not *here*. But I do think you ought to ask a question instead of just looking at the clock. It won't go away you know.'

He's got round gold glasses, long white hair, a clean-shaven wrinkled face and a pair of blue eyes that look me up and down very carefully.

'You shouldn't be wearing that wig,' he says. 'It makes it difficult for people to recognise you. And it really isn't necessary, not for what you are going to do. Where did you get it?'

'From the Queen. I mean the Queen of Witches. She told me *never* to go anywhere without one.'

'I wouldn't listen to *her*. We don't. Not here in New York. Here everyone only listens to themselves and that when they've got the time for it. And time is a terrible problem here.'

'Is that why the clock shows four different times?'

'Never mind the clock. The clock can't agree on anything. The four faces are always arguing. That's why you mustn't mind it. Just pretend it isn't there. Now for your question.'

'Is he here? The wizard I mean.'

'Why of course he is! He is at the top of the stairs. You have kept him waiting. And by the way, his name is Orlando.'

Wizards in my experience—and suddenly I've got experience and am full of a past I didn't even know I had—wizards like to appear at the top of stairs leading nowhere in particular. It's their sort of place. And Orlando is a wizard. I know that—as you do in dreams where things tangle and untangle, taking the dreamer with them in their flow.

'Annabel,' shouts the wizard. 'I have been waiting so long I nearly raided the food-halls. My God what food-halls! The Queen of Witches is down there selling cucumbers at a dollar a dozen and she's as grumpy as grumpy can be. The Duchess of Dronymore is there with a basket on her arm, the size of a lion, as if she wanted to buy the place.'

'With her everything is the size of a lion.'

'Lions you know,' says Orlando thoughtfully. 'Lions

really deserve more respect than that, but try telling that to the duchess. Lions….' Now he is shouting and pointing and I can see a lion on its haunches, cross-pawed and casual asking about the times for a train. It's got no mane, so it's a lioness.

'Everyone needs a train,' says the wizard. 'And I think we should take one. Tell the lioness there you that you've got the tickets and she needn't worry about the train times. They're all wrong anyway, because they try to follow the clock.'

I tell the lion that I've got the tickets. She looks me up and down.

'Rubbish,' she says, closing her eyes. 'You mean the wizard has got them. Wizards have always got tickets, but you can't trust them to take you anywhere *you* want to go. At heart, they're all control freaks and go where their fancies take them, but I'm my own man or my own lioness. Always have been. Nobody can tell me anything, not in this world or in any other.'

She looks wise and I know that I ought to stick to her, because she's more reliable than a wizard, even if she does have a mighty roar and one she's busy trying out. It fills the hall like a blast of wind through a wood, nearly pushing one over. I can see people running and falling over one another. Within a few seconds the great hall is almost empty. The lioness lowers her head and whispers, 'this is part of the plan. That roar was part of the plan. Good wasn't it?'

And I know the plan without her telling me. I have got this special feeling about what is happening. They have got a plan. And the plan is to steal the clock. How they are going to do it, I don't know, not yet. That is still hidden, but what is happening is bad enough.

'The duchess wants the clock,' says the lion. 'And anyway it's not much good here.'

'Sure you aren't stealing it for yourself?'

'You understand a thing or two, but it doesn't add up to much,' says the lioness. 'That's the way it is with human beings. All show and no fandango. By the way I didn't tell you my name.'

'Please do.'

'Annabel,' whispers the lioness. 'I am the first Annabel. Fifteen to go, but I doubt you'll make it.'

Again she roars and this time it's such a mighty roar, the wizard is swept off the stairs in a gust of wind. A moment later, I follow. A great tongue of air sweeps us along. One moment, we are brushing against the walls, another looking at the ceiling. I am closing my eyes to avoid seeing too many things rush past me, but I can feel them and hear them. I'm holding onto my wig.

'All show,' repeats the lioness. 'And no fandango. Now you know what I think.'

As she closes her mouth, I slip down suddenly from my latest height (somewhere close to the ceiling) and find myself—why, in a train, of course. I know it's a train before I even open my eyes because of the sound of the wheels on the track.

'We had to speed things up,' explains the wizard. 'Or we would have been there all day. That's why I asked her to roar. She's got such a mighty roar. It's the best thing about her. Have you been there before?' He doesn't give me time to answer. 'Grand Central, I mean. It's a wicked place, one of the wickedest I know, and I'm a wizard. Annabel, the lioness, is mad about it. She's even fallen in love with the clock, though she won't admit it. All that nonsense about the duchess wanting it is just lies. She wants it for herself. She is always falling in love with clocks and that's something I can't understand, this love of something that isn't magic, and just goes round and round. Why, it doesn't change from one year to the next. It's just something to put somewhere. She's got a cave full of them, but this one is the jewel, the jewel in the crown. She has been walking up and down Grand Central, admiring it for days. She is determined to steal it, you know. Quite determined.' He closes his eyes. His hands are resting on his lap, one on top of another. I try to imagine all the things he can do with those wizard hands, but for now he's asleep. I have got lots of time to look around. It's an old carriage with velvet seats and tiny windows that look difficult to open because of their metal fastenings. Everywhere there is dust and dirt, as if the train had been going up and down these tracks, up and down, from place to place, for a very long time.

Everything feels so weird because I'm *inside* a story. Yes, all around me there is *story*, like water or air, there's no getting away from it. I'm like a fish in the sea, or a diver, first time exploring the seabed where he's never been before. Where things have their own comings and goings. It's a strange place all right, even without a wizard fast asleep, snoring right opposite me. Snore, snore, snore, like my grandmother, like all old people, who seem to tumble into sleep like babies and into an old, old face made of leather and sprouting hair, folds loosely arranged around an opening, the mouth. More a landscape than a face; the mouth bubbling sound like a small volcano.

'Orlando, wake up!' I shout. I've had enough, quite enough.

'Clocks,' he whispers, still asleep. 'Clocks. What can a lion do with clocks? A thousand and one clocks, at least. Well, you can ask my giddy aunt. The blessed lion can't even tell the time without counting her toes and her whiskers. She goes to pieces if it isn't bang on the hour. Tried her once on a quarter past three. Couldn't do it. Couldn't do it if her life depended on it. Couldn't do it, couldn't do it.'

'Orlando, wake up!'

'Couldn't do it. I wake, when I wake. Take the key, if

you want it. It's got your name on it. I would take it. Always take things with your name on it. That's my advice.' The snoring continues.

Lying loosely in his hands, there's a key, I hadn't noticed. *Annabel's key*, it says on a piece paper attached by a string. 'For opening things, when it's appropriate. When it's right.'

The carriage rattles and the doors bang. We are moving so fast I can barely make out what's outside the window: hills, fields and animals, some big, some small. Might be sheep and cows or might be —I look closer— something else entirely, like unicorns. Anyway it's a bit of a blur.

'What does it mean 'appropriate or the right time'? How can I know when it's the right time or the right door?' I'm really angry. I think I've had enough of this story. The key looks venomous. Before I can think, I have shaken him, and hard.

Grabbing hold of me with his strong arms, fully awake, he smiles.

'That is what you *never* know. Not until you have done it, until you've opened it. But if you've got it wrong, then the goblins and hobgoblins will get you. There you are. That's a fact and there's nothing you can do about it. Absolutely nothing, and I wouldn't try to be clever, it never works.'

'That's not very helpful.'

'You are used to advice being helpful—but here it is confusing and creepy. That's the way it is in the land of magic. Anyone asked for our tickets yet?'

Awake, he's a different man, and his age suits him. It goes with being a wizard and makes him awesome now that he's slipped out of sleep and stopped that mad snoring. His face and neck are full of rivers, but his nose is strong and smooth, his mouth a clean slit. He sweeps his forehead with one of his huge hands, awake and at the ready. Ready to grab and hold tight. His eyes are nestling purposefully in their sockets. A pair of spies who have worked together for longer than I've been alive. He wouldn't be wondering whether he'd seen sheep or unicorns. He *knows* what he sees. Every bit of him is awake. This old body is just something for him to lurk inside, a wizard's hiding place. I wonder what mad reason made me grab and shake him. He's a wizard, after all. I should be more careful, but careful is something I don't know anymore, now that I'm in the land of magic, now that I've become part of a story. *Careful* belongs somewhere else.

'You are a special person,' he says, as if reading my thoughts. 'You have shaken a wizard and that *could* be a bad thing. I would be careful, if I were you. You might not get away with it next time. Let's see what has fallen out of my pockets, if any magic has escaped. Anything you like, is yours. Finders keepers. But I would be careful, if I were you.'

'More creepy advice.'

'You can take it or leave it,' he smiles. 'Like all advice.'

On the floor lies a whole load of things. He must have had a crazy amount in his pockets. They must have been bulging like mountains. Strange, I never noticed.

'There we are,' he says, pointing carelessly. 'What a lot of stuff. I know several hobgoblins who would give their eyes and teeth for this, if only they could. This is magic to die for. Proper magic, fantastic magic, magic that could make the world go round for a thousand years or more, if only it's put to good use. There's a riot of adventure here, and for the taking. God bless you little Miss Annabel, because there's more here than you've bargained for, that I can tell you. Choose carefully. Or, as they say, the goblins will get you.'

It is all spread out, the weird and the wonderful and the really ordinary, a small wave of things on the floor. I bend down; the pile seems to grow one minute and shrink the next.

'When you take one thing, something else disappears. If I were you, I would hurry up. They are magic things and don't wait for anyone. My, you've got eyes the size of saucers, but if I were you, I would do more than just look. The more you take, the more vanishes and some times more things vanish than you have taken. There's no knowing, so you better get on with it.'

I take a coin and a key disappears. Down on my knees

I grab what I can, filling my lap with things as others are sucked away. The dirty windows sift segments of light onto the floor, but I can't see as well as I would like. Besides I'm in a hurry. What did the wizard say? Here's magic to die for. Quickly, I grab what I can off the floor.

'Well, well,' he says. 'Some good things and some bad things. Not entirely the choice I would have made, but finders keepers. Show me what you've got.'

'Two coins.'

'Good to pay with. I see they've got dragons on them.'

'Does that matter?'

'Everything matters. But it's too late to think about that now.'

'Three keys.'

'A silver one, a gold one and a copper one. To be used with the right doors.'

'The wrong ones and the goblins will get me.' I look him straight in the eye. I am getting the hang of this and no longer feel afraid. Goblins and hobgoblins—you wait! I've got magic on my side—well some magic, it may be wrong magic but I have a sense of luck, a deep sense of *power*. I've shaken a wizard, and you're not the same person after that. Not the same person at all.

'The wrong ones and the goblins or hobgoblins will get me,' I repeat. There's strength in my voice.

'That's the general idea, the general direction of things,' he says smiling. 'There are local variations, of course. My, my, five minutes into a story and haven't we grown up, aren't we proud! Well, let's see how long that will last. I'm an old wizard and I've seen a thing or two. What have you got there?'

'Looks like a bit of fluff.' I can't help laughing. 'A bit of fluff, a small ball of wool, two feathers, a badge of sorts, a beetle and a frog.'

'You've struck lucky,' he says. 'I think you've struck lucky there.'

The frog looks up at me while the beetle scurries down my leg. Quickly I catch it and put it in my pocket with everything else. The frog goes in last. It feels soft and I mustn't squash it. I know it's special.

'What are you doing with that? I would put it under your wig if I were you. A much better place for a frog. Never put a frog in your pocket. Under your wig—that's where it belongs, along with the beetle of course. That's probably why she told you to wear it—to have somewhere to put things. Human beings have no common sense. No common sense at all. But witches do—they are bristling with it. Always listen to a witch.'

'How can I get them out again?'

'Just whistle for them. Annabel beetle, Annabel frog.' He whistles gently.

The whistle grows louder and the train seems to be slowing down. The beetle and the frog must have jumped under my wig because I can feel something there. There's a gentle scratching of feet, ten of them there must be. I look round for the wizard. He seems to be vanishing. His body has already become part of the air and his head is floating.

'You're on your own now,' whispers the head looking at me kindly. 'Good luck. You'll need it. You'll really need that when you are in the *Great Hall*, but never forget you've met a wizard, a fine wizard, and a great wizard. One of the greatest of them all. Orlando is my name. Don't forget it.'

'Orlando,' I shout at what's left of him, his hat, his eyes, his mouth, his nose and his shoes—what a way he has of vanishing! 'Orlando!' I shout. 'What am I to do with your name?'

'Don't know,' he whispers gently. 'Don't know really, but I think there'll be something you can do with it, and when that happens, it will be the most natural thing in the world. Anyway, the name of a wizard is a powerful thing. Always has been, always will be.'

As he speaks the last words, he is gone. I am all alone in the train.

'Tickets,' shouts a large toad in a shiny green uniform covered in gold buttons. 'Tickets.' His big eyes are looking at me patiently. He seems to have all the time in the world and he has kind smile.

'Tickets, young lady. Have you got your tickets?'

'Only the one, here it is.'

'And the beetle and the frog? They travel free, I suppose. Well, never mind. I'm feeling generous. Want to blow bubbles?'

Out of his pocket he takes a small container, dips and blows, his huge lips tunnel shaped, his eyes fixed on a bubble that keeps growing and growing till it is almost the size of him, that giant toad, standing proudly with his feet splayed. An enormous rainbow bubble nearly fills the compartment.

'There,' he says pointing. 'If you look inside you can see the cave of the clocks, the kingdom of Annabel the lioness. Well, well – wonderful isn't it? Grandifolous,

magnifolous and splendifolous, wouldn't you say? What do you think?' He gives the bubble a gentle tap with one of his long toes so that it floats towards the window where it's caught and starts to change shape becoming long and flat. I look into it before disappears, out of the train, lost in a gush of wind. There she is, Annabel in her cave. Wow, what a cave.

In the cave of the clocks there is a ticking and striking of the hour and the half hour and the quarter. The noise is constant. Annabel the lioness lies on a large shelf formed by the rock, head cupped in one of her strong paws, listening. There's a lot to hear: tinkling, gonging, ringing, any number of ways of marking the hour, including the mellow ding-dong of old bells. It is a vast cave, still it feels cramped because there are clocks everywhere: big clocks, small clocks, wooden and metal clocks, grandfather and grandmother clocks, clocks that work in strange ways and are made of unexpected things. Some beautiful, some hideous, some weird and wonderful. Beneath a small moonfaced clock with two dragon tails as hands, lies Annabel now asleep and dreaming. Dreaming of what? Of grand Central Station, I am sure and *that* clock. She wants it hanging high above her, close to her chandelier which is made of crystal and has a hundred branches. Yes, that is where the Tiffany clock from Grand Central Station is meant to be. That is where it is going to hang. She has got a chain and hook ready.

She is dangling them in her sleep, her dreaming face full of mischief.

That's what I see, all in that bubble, before it floats out of the window and disappears.

'Wonderful isn't?' says the toad. 'I wish I had such a way with stealing, such magic in my fingers, such tinkling in the fingertips, such…' he pauses, looking round as if he might find a word or two floating in the air. 'Such,' he unwraps the word slowly triumphantly—to me it's nothing but sound, 'such presti-digi-tation.' He leans back. 'My grandmother taught me that word. 'Beware,' she used to say, 'beware of prestidigitation. It means quick fingers. Boy, has that lioness got quick fingers. She's awesome and so cool—the coolest lioness in the world.'

'Do you always talk like this? My head is spinning with *prestidigitation*.'

'Always,' says the toad sadly. 'But sometimes more so. Want another bubble?' Not waiting for an answer, he blows and there she is inside the bubble, the Queen of Witches herself, looking me straight in the eye. For a moment the bubble rests on the windowpane. Then it is gone.

'Feeling melancholy?' asks the toad. 'I would if I were you. It helps, you know. Melancholy means sad, just a weeny bit sad. It's what gives my eyes their shape and it makes me want to talk. But don't be too sad,' he laughs.

'The Queen of Witches hasn't got you yet, but don't forget the hat, you know. Don't forget to bring her that hat, that gobsmacking hit-you in-the-eye hat, the one she's waiting for, the hat, the hat, the hat...'

His voice is trailing. What is he saying? His words seem all tangled up and they mingle with the noise of the train. 'Sad, you know,' he says at last. 'It's a good thing to be. Sad and phantasmagorical, if you know what I mean...'

I look at him—what fine toad eyes. Behind him stretches the train, one single long compartment, and the more I look, the longer it grows. A long tunnel with specks of light from the windows. There is a small square of darkness at the far end which seems to suck my toad into it, swallowing him up in a whoosh of air, but I can still hear him whispering, 'phantasmagorical, smorical, borical. You know what I mean, phantasmagorical, phantasmo...' Then it's all gone, and the sound of the train has stopped. Underneath my legs I can feel something soft. Leaves, I think. Yes, I'm in a wood surrounded by trees and I can really hear the wind. I can feel something too. Something live under my wig. The two Annabels.

I am at the end of a path, in a small clearing in a wood of beech and oak with a sprinkling of chestnut. Mighty old trees, their branches high above the ground shimmering with specks of light. What did the toad say? *Phantasmagorical*, I think it was. And in response to my thoughts, there is the toad's voice, 'Phantasmagorical, smorical, borical, don't forget that now. Phantasmagorical, now that's a good word and you'll need it one day. You'll need it when you are faced with the mad, the bad and the ugly. It will come in hand, it will. That and a hat. Don't forget the hat.' The leaves tremble as the whisper passes through them, but suddenly it's all over. Silence.

'Nothing,' I tell myself out loud. 'Nothing can happen here. Absolutely nothing.'

Through the wood comes a whisper, a very gentle whisper as if someone were in a hurry to say something that had been left out, 'phantasmagorical, all phantasmagorical in the wood with a queen—a wicked, a wicked queen.' The whisper stops and I am just about to tell myself not to listen to it, when I notice someone coming down the path. It is *her*. Yes, you can't mistake her.

It is the queen herself, the Queen of Witches! I have never seen her before, but do I know who she is! That nose, those eyes, that stare, and that way of flexing her eyebrows as if they might bend the world. Goodness, she looks like a cross between an empress and a mad woman, with a bit of magic and darkness thrown in, a touch of evil. She's talking to herself and I, of course, am listening. I wish I had my notebook and pen, though I know you must never write down what a witch is saying. Never. Not ever. But who could resist this babbling queen coming headlong down the path, hair flying and wicked thoughts in the air?

'I will not,' she's saying. 'I will not hear of it! Certainly not. That flibbertigibbet thinks she can do whatever she wants and get away with it. No Siree.' She stops, she looks round.

'Don't you agree, young lady?'

I am not saying a word. I have had my fill of speaking to witches. You have to be so careful of them. They seem to have feelings everywhere, like the tentacles of an octopus so you never know where you are stepping.

'Well, wouldn't you agree?'

'Depends.'

'What do you mean depends? Either someone *is* a flibbertigibbet or they are something *else*. And you have to make up your mind, *and* you have to do it quickly. Anyway, she *thinks* she can do what she wants and get *away* with it. So she must be a flibbertigibbet. End of story.'

I find myself nodding my head.

'She's got the clock, you know, and she thinks that is awfully clever, really awesome. Well, perhaps it is just a teeny-weeny bit clever, if you like that sort of thing. I mean wingle wangling it like that, hiding it among my cucumbers in the darkness of the night. Then stealing down softly on her paws before day light and whisking it away in a big black trunk! Well, I'll grant you that, it's a clever thing all right, specially when you think of all the police and the security. I mean, this is New York and

Grand Central! And no one seeing anything. Even less suspecting a lion. Well, on the other hand, why should they? Do you ever think to yourself, 'well, maybe a lion's taken it?' You've heard of a lion's share, of course. But I can tell you something. Yes, you can take it from me, the Queen of Witches. Lions don't share. Never ever. And that's the problem with this lion: she won't share her clock.'

Aha, so that's what it's about: the clock. It's gone from Grand Central Station. Annabel, the lioness, has made it vanish into thin air. I can imagine all those people there gawping, their eyes scanning everything above them, not believing what they are seeing, or failing to see. They find themselves looking again and again. Surely it must be there? Why there are some things that just don't happen, they just don't, because they are not possible. But the clock has gone.

'How did she do it?'

'Not quite sure. It was bolted down, but she has a way with her paws and some cream she uses in difficult situations. She must have shrunk it a bit before she put in her bag. She has a marvellous way with slipping things inside bags. Pure magic, I would say and I know a thing or two about that.' Out of breath she sits down next to me.

'And now it's in her cave?'

'Not sure about that. You saw that bubble a few moments ago, didn't you? The one the toad blew with her cave in it? Well, she was lying in her cave waiting and thinking, a chain in her paw, planning where she might hang it and savouring her moment of decision. She looked like a lion with a trick or two up her sleeve, if you ask me. And it would look so good in Witch Hall, which is *my* hall and the finest place in the world. Witch Hall,' she says closing her eyes, dreaming. 'Witch Hall is made of rock and daubing—magnificent daubing. It looks as if a galaxy or two had been trapped inside it and light bounces off it in the way that only light knows how to bounce. Oh, it's the most wonderful place in the world is Witch Hall but there isn't a clock there to seen. Not one. And time there passes ever so slowly sometimes. It just rolls itself up and goes to sleep.'

She is smiling and I have never seen a witch smile before. Well, not the Queen of Witches.

'I want that clock,' she says. 'And I do think, I'll get it. I always travel hopefully. That's why they made me queen. Want a chocolate? I have got a bag full.'

She waits for me to nod and then bursts out laughing.

'You haven't been here long, have you?'

I shake my head.

'Well, never say *yes* to anything before asking the vital question: is it magic? Because you never know about magic. It can be good, bad, nothing much, and pure *evil*. Pure *sparkling evil*. And you want to know first—beggars must be choosers—that's my motto. Well, there is no magic in these chocolates, none at all. But they taste damn good. I made them myself from the finest choco-late in the world that just happens to grow in my garden. I'll show you, if you want, when you come to Witch Hall. Meanwhile, have a chocolate. They're all the same, so don't waste your time choosing.' She looks at me with those wicked eyes.

I put one it in my mouth where it melts deliciously. I'm closing my eyes in pure delight when I feel something happening on the ground. I look down. My feet are growing and seem to be heading for a bush I hadn't noticed before.

'Tricked you!' shouts the queen. 'Never trust a witch. You can't do that in a month of Sundays.'

I eyes are fixed on my feet. My toes seem to have developed a life of their own and are slipping through the grass on their way to somewhere. When will they stop? You never know about magic.

'Lucky your shoes seem to be growing as well,' says the queen. 'They'll stop in a moment. Don't worry, my dear. Your feet won't go far. They can't, if you think about it. Always keep calm, and panic as a last resort. Try sitting down and putting them in the air. They won't like that and might stop.'

I do as she tells me. It's nice among the tall grass with, my feet high above my head. I'm not worried. Perhaps I've already got used to magic.

'There,' says the queen in a kind whisper. 'Look,

they've stopped growing. I said they would. Now about that clock.'

'What about it?'

'I must have it.'

She smiles but there is something wicked about her. Those big green eyes, horrible eyebrows, high forehead, firm thin lips and that way of looking at you so that you forget about everything, except her eyes.

'Is this the first time you have tried magic, tried it on yourself, I mean?' she asks.

I nod. I have seen magic but this is the first time it's happened to *me*. I am just a little proud and I am thinking to myself, 'you are part of a story now, Annabel. You are part of a story and *anything* could happen. You are sitting in the grass with toes like towers and speaking to the Queen of Witches. So there, Annabel!'

'Don't think you can get used it,' says the queen, as if she were reading my thoughts. 'No one does, you know. Magic always takes you by surprise. There is usually something about it, you really *do* mind, even if you pretend not to. You do mind your nose, don't you? I wouldn't of course, but then witches don't mind noses. I wouldn't mind your nose. Not all. Though it would look silly on a *small* witch.'

My nose. Yes, there is something sticking out from my face and it is *not* something familiar. Not entirely. What length, what texture, what a feel it has.

'Not bad,' says the queen. 'You could just pass for a witch now. All you need is a familiar. I think you have got one already. What's underneath that wig?'

'Two Annabels,' I reply. 'Two mad Annabels. A beetle and a frog and they are both called Annabel. I keep them underneath my wig and I can feel them creeping and crawling round my head. It feels nice, once you are used to it.'

'Gives you courage, I bet. You wouldn't be talking to me, the Queen, if you didn't have two familiars for company. As they say in that wicked place where they used to keep that clock, you can bet your bottom dollar. Yes, you really can.'

'Do you go there often?'

'New York,' she says dreamily. 'Can't say I go there often, but I'm there from time to time, when the fancy takes me. I always let my feelings be my guide. Saw the clock and fell in love with it. Sometimes I sell cucumbers or bagels down below. Well, you will have to help me get that clock for Witch Hall, if you want your nose back, or if you want to fit into human-size shoes again.'

Out of her pocket she takes a silver mirror in the shape of a small moon decorated with snakes with beady red eyes and sharp, green tongues.

'Ready to admire yourself?'

There it is and no one can miss it, a nose Pinocchio would be proud of. Long and sharp like a pencil. I'm wearing a blond wig that sweeps down to my shoulder. To my amazement, I don't look in the least embarrassed. No, far from it, my face seems completely at home in its new splendour and I wonder whether there is a different brain lurking inside the girl in the mirror. Doesn't she know what she looks like? Where did she find that wig? I am about to look away when something catches my attention: the wig is moving. A strange bulge is making a journey across my forehead, pushing aside a mop of hair and emerging gloriously. There she is, my familiar, Annabel frog with the beetle big on her back. The queen snaps the mirror shut.

'Like what you saw? Too late to do anything about it. Not right now, anyhow; but if you can lay your hands on that clock, then I might do something about your nose. In Witch Hall we need a clock and that's the one I want—it's wicked and the coolest thing on the planet. I *must* have it. I need it for my spells because some of them are so particular about time. All sorts of time—the time to do things, to say all those magic words. Rimple, rample, blood, brain, bone, wiggle, waggle roar, fi-fi-fo-fum..' She closes her eyes dreamily. 'And then there's the time to strike the huge gong that's in Witch Hall and has been there as far back as anyone can remember. That's the best time of all, gong time. Just let it roar!' Her eyes grow big.

'It's the size of a bath tub, but the shape of a cauldron,

and it stands in the middle of the hall, commanding attention which it certainly gets because everyone who enters Witch Hall can't take their eyes off it, or the throne right behind it. Not for a second, not even enough of a second for a bat to blink as it skims through the air.

The gong rests on six dragons made of metal. When you strike it, a shiver runs through their tails and their eyes blaze. That's magic of course, but nothing compared to the sound which runs all around the hall, carrying a thousand echoes, sending ripples through the stone walls and stone floors. You feel as if the world was made of sound and some monster was the musician. A rich tempest of whirling noise makes Witch Hall tremble. There is no finer feeling than that sea of sound, moving slowly from the striking of the gong, rippling out till the walls hear it and send it back; back and forth till it stops and there is silence, an awesome silence and perfect for spells and wickedness. Pure wickedness. I'm addicted to that, you know. The dragons close their eyes and then the magic begins. There is nothing like it. Nothing in the world and I know the world, I can tell you, because I have been even further than New York, having sold my cucumbers in far flung places that you wouldn't have dreamt of because we witches are devilishly curious and think the world a place to be seen and travelled. Selling vegetables is something you can do anywhere. I'm into cucumbers because you can pack them up easily and no one notices the seller, because no one cares that much about cucumbers. So I stand behind my box of cucumbers—hands on, burning with wickedness—but no one notices. And I have done that from the foot of the Himalayas and great plains of Africa to nowhere in particular. I have watched the wildebeest leaping and listened to elephants trumpeting and stamping while standing there offering cucumbers to whoever wants to buy. I've had wonderful times, I can tell you, but it's nothing like doing magic in Witch Hall and sending things flying. Now that beats everything else in the world.'

Suddenly she is silent. Her green eyes are on me and I can't help thinking of the poor Wask. Imagine being pursued by one of those eyes night and day and with no witch behind it—a detached witch eye on the loose and with a purpose.

'But for good magic, I need a clock,' she whispers dreamily. 'Magic is very particular. Pure evil is something different.'

'Is it?' I ask, not wanting to know, but those eyes are forcing me to speak, making me ask questions, no one would want to ask.

'Yes,' she replies. 'Well up to a point,' she adds thoughtfully. 'There is no knowing with *Pure Evil*. I have got *Pure Evil* right here. I keep it in my pocket and I'll let it lose, unless I can have my fun with magic. I want magic—my fingers are trembling to make Witch Hall shake and shiver with the gonging and the magic running through the Hall like a whoosh of wind through a forest, catapulting the birds from their nests and branches and sending the mice scurrying. Once I get started, the bats will be out of the belfry, the chandeliers swinging on their chains the length of the Hall, and there is no stopping *me*. But I do need a clock and that's the one I want. So get it for me or *Pure Evil* is on the loose.'

'What can it do when it's on the loose?' I ask nervously.

'Do you need to know? Do you *want* to?' She looks at me with those eyes. Majestically, she turns her back on me and walks down the path which seems to grow in response to her firm steps. She is one, all must obey. She is the queen. Suddenly the path stops, she has gone. All I can hear is some pigeons cooing. The frog has jumped down and is in front of me. The beetle is sitting on his head, looking at me curiously.

'We will have to get it,' says the frog simply. 'We will have to get that clock.'

Maxim is smiling, 'You're in one hell of a story, Annabel,' he is saying. 'One mess of a story and there is no knowing whether you will get out of it.'

They are all sitting around me listening. You could hear the pitter patter of a mouse in the All Night Diner, that's how quiet it is. I can see the duchess, face cupped in her hand, and Roland, the familiar of familiars, a dozen small trolls, and a bevy of witches. They are all listening and there is no danger that the goblins or hobgoblins will get me, but there are worse creatures than goblins. I can feel a growing sense of danger rising inside me like a wave.

'Does it sometimes happen,' I ask anxiously. 'Does it sometimes happen that someone never gets out of a story?'

Maxim shakes head his sadly. 'Yes, that happens all the time. Sometimes people just get swallowed up whole and you never see them again. Not ever. They just swirl round and round in the bowels of a story, as if they had been eaten by a dragon. So you better get that clock, I warn you. By the way, it is her birthday and I would give her a present, if I were you.'

'But what shall I bring her? What can you give someone who's into magic and the queen of witches?'

'A hat,' says the duchess. 'Ever seen a witch without a hat? Witches collect them like some people collect shoes. They just can't get enough of them. And there is never any magic in the hat. It's the only thing without magic. Witches can have magic even in their toes, but not in their hats. Yet they are crazy about them and will go to any length to get one, if they really, really want it. I once knew a witch who spent the afternoon crouched inside a letterbox waiting for a woman with a splendid hat to post a letter, just so that she could grab the hat. It was a black and yellow one with two mice dangling by their tails out of the jaws of a crocodile. The crocodile was small, but its jaws were huge. On either side of the croc were two huge spiders, busy weaving these bright yellow nets that covered most of the hat. I have never seen anything like it. Not the kind of thing that suits everyone and I wouldn't wear it myself, but this witch was mad for it, and once she got her long witch claws on it, she never let go. I've even heard that she sleeps with it on. That's what her familiar says. Once a witch wants something, she wants it. They have got devilish determination, as we all know.'

Looking pleased with all that knowledge, and the fact that it isn't her who has to get the clock and bring it to Witch Hall, the duchess laughs a deep throaty laugh, takes a grilled lizard from a nearby plate and lifts it proudly to her lips.

'Four hours and twenty minutes to go,' she whispers. 'Then it'll be midnight and the queen's birthday. You better get your skates on!'

Maxim puts his big warm paw on my shoulder and gives me a hug. Nothing like the hug of a troll to give you comfort, but I'm not sure it is enough to make me as brave, as I would like to be, as brave as this story deserves.

'Time to get on,' he says, reading my thoughts. 'I'll be thinking of you, but it's time to go. Can you hear the wind?'

There is a wind all right, and it's blowing straight

through Maxim's. Straight through the thick curtains it goes, bringing a host of leaves with it. Some of the familiars have to hold on to the tables to stay where they are. I just close my eyes. When I open them, I can see a building surrounded by towers on a hill far away. That must be Witch Hall. Even at a distance it looms mighty in the night, which has come upon this place so suddenly, it takes your breath away. This is some darkness. Ears at the ready to catch any sound, I stand still and wait. First I need to get the feel of things right here: there's the moon there on my left, its face hanging low among the branches of an aged oak where I can see a couple of owls lurking, and on my right the brow of a wood. Beyond it all, in the distance, there's Witch Hall. Its black towers seem painted onto the darkness of the night. Immediately in front of me, there is a path going this way and that. There is no logic to its twists and turns. Whoever designed it was mad: here it curls round a tree, there it tunnels its way straight through some bushes, only to loop lazily on the other side, giving a long view of nothing in particular. It hasn't made up its mind whether to be in a hurry. The owls are looking at me, but I don't have time for them. I'm thinking of what the duchess said: I need my skates on for midnight and the queen's birthday. There are things to be done. I'm all pins and needles, as eager as can be. This silence, this darkness excites. I haven't got time for owls. I want to leave them to their hooting, but then I hear one calling to another, 'Annabel, Annabel...'

My curse! I had almost forgotten my curse. How many Annabels have I got? Five, I can count, five Annabels. A lioness, a frog, a beetle and now, two owls. Eleven more to go before the clock strikes twelve and the wicked queen's party really begins! There is a snake on the path, asleep I think but, as I walk by, its tail turns live, hitting my heel. Facing its eyes, its tongue, its darts of motion, the courage in me dies a quicker death than I care to admit. I'm rooted to the spot.

'Are you an Annabel?' I whisper hopefully trying to make my courage return.

'Annabel, my sock! Like that paltry frog or that beetle or them two owls? Or that crazy lioness with her clock, her mad passion for clocks, any clock. A fine clock, a manky clock, it's all the same to that lioness, once she's got her eye on it, she wants it. She's been planning the great robbery on Grand Central for years, been sitting in her cave, tail swishing, planning it all. My, what a crazy lioness! Have you ever seen all her clocks? The cave is jim-jam packed with them and the noise is awesome. That lioness must be deaf, as well as mad.'

Silence. A shiver runs down the snake's back with the effort of all that talking and then it lies quite still, its length slung across the path in front of me. In the distance, I can see Witch Hall. Yes, that is definitely

Witch Hall. And she'll be waiting. The queen will be waiting for her clock. Is that snake looking at me? Suddenly I remember: snakes can't close their eyes. So perhaps it's asleep. It certainly isn't moving. I try prodding its tail, its head swirls round.

'Wizard,' I whisper. 'I know a wizard. He's called Orlando.'

The snake coils itself round my foot and lifts its head, impressed perhaps.

'Orlando himself. Well, well. The little girl knows Orlando. The wizard of wizards, and in his honour, I shall give you the hat of hats. For the queen of course. She's mad about hats. Come with me.'

He disappears along the path but I can hear a rustling of leaves. I don't find it difficult to keep up. My mad feet know the way; my witch's feet can trample right through bushes. They really know a thing or two and suddenly there I am, inside a tree. It's humongous and hollow to the very top so that there is space for bats to fly around. It is like being inside a church. There are candles in the hollows of the tree, a fine riot of shadows leaping everywhere. The wind is blowing through the cracks in the ancient trunk, making a low musical sound, a whispering tune. As I get used to the shimmering light, I can see things growing, pale leaves and dusty flowers. Spiders and beetles are at work.

'Take your pick of the hats. You know the name of a

wizard. Wouldn't have brought you here otherwise.'
Slowly the snake slides through a knotted opening in the
trunk and disappears.

In the centre of this lofty place, slung in a pile, there
are hats and hats galore. Sitting by them there is an
ancient hobgoblin with a face like carved wood.

'My work,' she says. 'All my work.'

That'll be the sixth I think to myself, the sixth Annabel.

'This is all my work.' Her voice is crackly and slightly
menacing. 'All my work. My lovely work. Days and
nights I sit here making hats. Hats which no one appre-
ciates or understands, though there is no magic involved,
no magic at all. It's just pure genius. Sinbad the sailor
taught me. He's sitting over there and he's on your side,
so you can have a hat.'

I remember Sinbad. I met him not that long ago in
Patrick's strange house where all of this began, but
nothing that's happened so far is a patch on this.

'Pure genius,' continues the hobgoblin. 'It's all pure
genius, but try telling that to anyone. This grubby crowd
of hobgoblins, trolls and witches, they are completely
taken in by magic, because it's got glamour, sudden
lights, bamboozling sound, as one thing explodes into
another. Wonderful, you might say. Well, up to a point.
Personally, I think magic is overrated and sometimes it
just boils down to something ordinary, a bit humsadasical, if you want my opinion. Take your nose. Good God

what a nose! Typical magic that. It's even got a few warts
—well that's magic for you. A lot of fandango, but what
you get is humsadasical. Who's impressed by a few warts
and lots of long?'

Every word is followed by a strange short hiss. I feel
my nose. Yes, it's a catastrophe. Pure catastrophe. But I
suspected that. Anyway, the queen promised she would
do something about that nose, once I've given her the
clock.

'Never mind my nose.' Do I sound like I don't care? I
hope so, but then I look at my feet.

'What a nose! Pleased with your feet? Those swirling
nails, those honky tonk toes? Well that's magic for you.
You can take it or leave it. Well, *you* can't of course. But
I can! Now look at the hats.'

The Hobgoblin bends over, her pointed chin touching
the pile, her claws searching deep inside it, her eyes like
lizards, scanning each hat.

'Here,' she shouts with quick certainty. 'Here it is, the
hat of hats. But I need payment.' She holds the hat up
high and the light falls on her wrinkled body. I can see
the shine of something on the hat but I can't quite make
it out. She puts it on the ground and holds a candle so
that I can admire her precious work. What a hat! There
is a black ship sailing across it, red sails billowing in a
magical wind. There are towers on a thin stretch of coast
so the ship has something to sail towards. And all of it is

covered in fine detail: there are spiders' webs in the tower windows, facing the ship and the sea. The waves roll in their own spray. There is even a gull catching a silver herring. There is no movement or sound, of course. There can't be. It isn't magic. Or is it? I'm not sure. No, there's no movement, no sound, no people either. Just more and more to see, every time you look. This is something beyond magic. Quickly, I put that silent world on my head.

'Have it,' she whispers. 'It is yours. Yours for better or for *worse*.' She laughs and her laughter dances round and round, echoed by the wooden walls. 'But I need some money. Nothing's for free, you know.' She bites her lip knowingly. I would be at a loss, but my familiar, Annabel the frog, finds the coins I got from the wizard. Well, that's what familiars are for, I suppose.

'Good,' she nods. 'I know those coins. They'll do. They've got dragons on them. That means you can trust them. And remember there are no dragons in New York.'

'No dragons?' I'm confused.

'No dragons. Hobgoblins, a few. Witches, occasionally. Trolls, rarely. But dragons never. There never have been, and never will be dragons in New York. Remember that. Time to go.'

A wind blows through and there is darkness. Complete and utter darkness and a strange silence. Why do I find a bit of silence more awesome than this blackness? I must get on; I feel an opening. Suddenly I know what to do: I rub the silver key on the trunk and I'm back on the road.

The road is nothing but a path, the time is night, my aim and purpose is Witch Hall which crowns the nearest hill, but first that wretched clock. I must get the clock or the queen might not be able to do her magic and will want to let lose *Pure Evil,* whatever that is. Not knowing what to do, I behave like any witch—and believe me with that nose, those feet I am any witch— and turn to my familiars.

'Annabel beetle, Annabel frog, can you help me— please, please?'

There's a rustling in my hat, the beetle is in the rigging and the frog is a captain with a telescope to one eye, looking very much in charge. But it is the beetle who speaks first.

'Make me bigger,' he says simply. '*Please*— just a little bigger. Well about the size of a dog. Doggy size will do because I deserve it and you can ride me then, like a real witch. Real witches love to ride beetles because of the stamp, stamp of our feet. That's style for you and I don't want to arrive at Witch Hall, a ming mong manky thing, just for people to step on. No, I want respect and to join in the fun, the fun of Witch Hall. The swish swash swoshing fun of the Great Hall itself, where anyone who is anything wants to be, because there the parties are real hard core and there is no end of dancing to that wicked

gong—the sound gets into your blood. Even the walls can't get enough. But *please* I need to be bigger. Just a lick of one of your feathers will do, the ones you got from the wizard, the king of wizards, Orlando himself. *Please.'*

I have learnt something new about witches: they are constantly being nagged by their familiars and this one is already getting on my nerves. Parties are all it can think of, while I have to do *all* the work and run the risks too. The parties in Witch Hall may be real hard core, but so are the dangers, what with the queen herself with pure *Evil* in her pocket, ready for use. But it's got me has this beetle and my brain is turning witch somersaults. It was talking about arriving in style, and style is a beetle if you are some kind of witch and haven't got anything better, like a dragon or a unicorn, or a sphinx that has lost its way. So I settle for my beetle and take a feather from my store of magical things. Swish, swosh, magic. The first time you do it, you feel like king of the universe, I can tell you. The beetle is the size of a horse.

'Take the other feather, you numbskull. Doggy size will do. I don't want to be too big for Witch Hall.'

Finally, we settle on something sensible, if you can call a beetle the size of a golden retriever a sensible thing. Carefully I mount.

Now let me describe my beetle because it deserves a few words to match its splendid looks, although I'll confess that it was perhaps more attractive when smaller, but that is only a bit of human bias, beetles not meant to be that big. Not in our world, anyhow, not in our experience, but now that I have done with all that's ordinary, I can kind of appreciate it. It's a fine creature really. At the front, there is something like a snout, with a pair of bright red antennae attached and a pair of beady eyes. Leaning over, I can see myself reflected in their black shields, nose, hat and all. There is the frog, still pretending to be a captain, as if this ship were more than a hat and could carry him across the seas. Behind the eyes, there is a polished plate of green, a cover for its back and two shiny wings. He's neatly balanced on six legs, bright orange with little clouds of black at their joints, ending in unexpected fury claws which you wouldn't think much good for running. This is Annabel beetle, and if style is what you want—but I won't go on because I have got things to do and there are imminent dangers ahead. The time is now—ten thirty—as the frog reminds me. She seems as dizzy as the beetle with the excitement of a trip to Witch Hall.

There it is looming in front of me, Witch Hall. I'm approaching at some speed, but first I must do a little detour to the cave of a lioness, the queen of stolen clocks. Annabel beetle tells me to hold on tight and remove my hat which she kindly hides under a wing, to keep it safe from the rip roaring wind. Through the forest we go, at a speed that would make a goblin take fright. Branches brush against my head. I shield my face by pressing my nose into the beetle's back. In a whirr we are there, coming to a sudden stop so that I fall off, right in front of a mysterious cave covered in ivy and moss. From inside comes the rumbling roar of a disappointed lioness. I'm not what she expected.

'Oh, it's you, is it?'

'It is,' I say proudly. 'I am Annabel, once a girl, but now a witch with a beetle and a frog, two familiars.'

'You didn't look so big, and carry yourself so proud when I saw you last, at Grand Central in New York.'

'I suppose I wasn't that big or so proud,' I say casually. 'I was new to the land of magic then. I hadn't met

Orlando the wizard, or grown a nose and a pair of feet to match.'

'Or worn a silly hat, for a silly, silly queen. The *Queen of Witches* is nobody to me and she can take her birthday and put it somewhere else—and her party too.'

The lioness is lying down in front of her cave, yawning carelessly as the clocks strike and continue striking. It's as if all the clocks in the world are in that cave—a mad, crazy whirl of sound. Tinkling, banging, gonging, it's all happening in there with a wisp of a lost cuckoo too. Has she got one of those too?

'Yes, I like them cuckoo clocks,' purrs Annabel in answer to my thoughts. 'Just one or two. You can get too much of them. I have pilfered them from the seven corners of the world, my clocks, my pride and joy. Just wait: there is even one that kind of yodels gently in your ear, just as you think it has all stopped. Just wait.'

But I don't have time for that. It's quarter to eleven now. Suddenly a little bit of inspiration comes my way. I have remembered something.

'What's the time?' I ask casually.

Well, that wipes the smile off her face.

'Who cares,' she roars but I know she doesn't mean it. I know how she's feeling when there is something you can't do, and it may be something useless, but you won't admit you can't do it—not for anything in the world. Annabel, the lioness who has stolen more clocks that anyone in this world and the next, can't tell the time. Round and round they all go, plotting something entirely mysterious to her, something she doesn't understand. She just lies there waiting for the sudden explosions of sound. Oh, I can teach you something, Annabel; in exchange for a little favour. And if you managed to winkle it out of Grand Central, why then you can easily get it back from Witch Hall. Its days there will only be numbered. The frog smiles. It's impressed, I can tell, because it has seen that lion's face. All I have to do now is to wait for that *yes* which I know will fall ripe and ready into my palm. Soon the lesson begins. Here is *one* and there is *two*. The beast can't count. 'It's what humans do,' she explains crossly. Humans and familiars. Witches can't or not as well as me, so I can't be a *real* witch. Slowly does it. Slowly, she learns the time. Finally, I make my way, the clock all wrapped up and made hand size by a feather's stroke.

And there it is in front of me: Witch Hall with its looming towers and moat. It is half past eleven and I am approaching at the double, doing a wild beetle ride. Oh, I've learnt a thing or two, being in this story. They can't stop me. Nobody can stop me. Two witches try to bar my way.

'I'm Annabel, come to see the queen and wish her happy birthday.' The beetle does a momentary stop and looks at the castle, big eyed. I know what she's thinking

'What's the code?' they whisper.

'There are no dragons,' I say firmly. 'No dragons...'

'Where?'

'In New York. There are no dragons in New York. Goblins a few, witches occasionally.' I'm warming to my subject, but they usher me through. Who can blame them: they're busy tonight. And there it is, the mighty door of Witch Hall gliding open to reveal the witches' feast in flickering candlelight. So many, I never thought I'd see so many candles: bronze holders stretch out their arms from the walls, a wealth of them and down from the ceiling hang metal mermaids with candles in their hair and tall torches in their hands. The place is alive with light and sound and I can hear the mighty gong. At the far end, the queen herself is dining on her throne waited on by hobgoblins and a couple of toads, the size of cats. I know I must go to her.

'You're here,' she whispers. 'How many Annabels?'

'Six: a frog, a beetle, two owls, a lioness and a hobgoblin who makes hats.'

'You're ten short! Over there, in the corner gossiping, you can see three witches with red hair. They're Annabels, all right. And by the door an old, old goblin dressed smartly in green. That toad,' she points. 'That toad is an Annabel, and there is spider on your left toe. Remember Mrs Rainbow said that you had to search high and low? Just below the ceiling, can you see those three snakes curled round the the mermaids? That's nine more Annabels, but you're still one short. And you know what that means! Have you got anything to say?'

Something trickles down my spine: no, I don't. Knowledge has deserted me, left me in the lurch. Fifteen Annabels, one short. That's the way it is in stories, in real stories. They get you in the end, somehow.

'There are no dragons,' I begin, not knowing what to say.

'Shut up,' hisses the queen. 'Who cares about what there is and isn't in New York? This is Witch Hall!'

My beetle has vanished and so has the frog. Around the gong there is wild dancing going on, witches and trolls flying in the air, a blur of colour dazzling the eye. But there is an ominous puddle of nothing happening round the queen's throne, a silence with a suppressed roar. Her eyes are on *me*. It's wicked. I know how the Wask felt.

'Got any presents?' She hits me with a question. I remember the hat, the glorious hat, but where is it? The beetle has got it, but Annabel beetle is no longer to be seen—she must be where the party's really going, stamping her six orange feet surrounded by a swirl of witches.

'A hat,' I mutter. 'I had a hat. I had...'

'Who,' shouts the queen. 'Who has taken my HAT. MY HAT!'

Silence cuts the air. The queen stands up and looks round.

'Who has taken my hat? My birthday hat, the work of

the best hobgoblin in the land. No magic, just the real McCoy. My hat!'

Slowly, antennae on the ground, eyes lowered, there she is, my beetle, my wacky familiar, and from under her wing she lets it slip to the ground, and here it is: the hat. The finest hat in the world and fit for a queen. Like lightning she grabs it in and places it on her head.

'Bring me a mirror,' she cries. 'I must have a mirror. My grandmother had one somewhere. On that wall behind the curtains and the crown which I never wear anyway, that's where it should be.'

Two witches hold the mirror for the Queen.

'Good,' she says. 'That is good. A fine ship, an awesome sight. That's wicked, you know,' she winks. 'And I know the meaning of that word, better than anyone in this room. A thousand and one witches, that's how many we are. Now where's the clock?'

I lift up its black covering and make it big, so BIG.

'Now we'll hang it,' says the queen. 'And then the fun will begin. Two minutes to twelve.'

I feel my nose, survey my feet. What's going to happen to me?

'You're one Annabel short,' she laughs, and what a wicked laugh. 'One Annabel short. Fifteen, but you need sixteen. So for the moment I'm forgetting about you, you can keep that nose and those toes. Now the fun will begin. Now it's time for the gong.'

There's a rush of wind, the hall trembles and I can hear the mighty gong. The queen stands high and lifts her hands in the air...

'That's some story,' says Maxim quietly. 'Some story.'

I'm back in Maxim's All Night Diner. They are all listening, their faces cupped in their hands. Goblins, trolls, hobgoblins, witches too.

'What's going to happen to me,' I whisper, aware that something is very wrong.

'I don't know,' replies Maxim, 'You're one Annabel short, so you may be well and truly stuck.'

'Stuck in a story?' I try to sound amazed, angry, indignant, but I know it's possible. Everything is possible.

'It's happened before, unfortunately. I remember once...' He smiles suddenly. 'But there is hope you know. Where is Mrs Rainbow?'

From the back of the hall I hear a rustling. Mrs Rainbow herself, broad and firm, is standing up.

'Well,' she says. 'The night is long but it's time to go, I think. The stars are quite pale now. So here I am. The sixteenth Annabel. If the queen will accept that, all is well. But she might not, you know. I'm not really part of the story and the clock has struck twelve.'

'Time to go,' shouts Maxim that big hairy troll. 'Time to go now, witches and familiars and all you creatures that come to my Diner. It's enough stories for one night.'

The waitresses hang up their roller skates and the kitchen is quiet, but I can hear other noises: the marching wolards are somewhere around and just faintly, there's the sound of a gong. Someone is also singing a song. 'When the world was a very young thing, and I was a fool of a troll.' A strong voice in the night. It is Maxim's, his deep troll voice. Something about the lies he used to tell and the witches he used to tell them to and how they would all listen in those wild, wild woods.

'I'm not sure,' says Mrs Rainbow. 'I'm really not sure you are going to escape. I'm not even sure that you *want* to, you know. You've been bewitched, all right, haven't you?'

Now that's a question! What a question but I've no time for it because my ears are hearing and my eyes are looking and it will answer itself anyhow, as most questions do. But for now it's time to go. Down the long, long road which leads from our All Night Diner to a couple of winks and a bit of sleepy eye in the Great Hall itself, or some other place that I may find because I am travelling light *and* hopefully, like the queen herself. And there is a word in my head, a word being whispered in my ear, like a potion being poured: *phantasmagorical*. Yes, it's *phantasmagorical* alright, this place, this wind, this moon, this mood in my head. Pure magic. Yes, and I am here and I want more. Come, you witches, come—there are things to be done. Things to be done. All around me the story swirls— this is only the beginning. By the side of the road I can see a large beetle lying as if discarded by the goings on of the night, empty of all energy it lies there snoring, furry legs folded, its head polished by the moon light. Yes, that party must have been real hard core…

About the author

Mikka was born in Denmark. As a child, she lived in Spain, Italy and Denmark but she has spent most of her adult life in London. She has written two novels, Gabriel's Bureau and The Dream Maker, both published by Dedalus but this is her first book for children. She enjoys travelling, listening to people talk, discovering new stories and fresh ways of telling them. She collects masks, loves theatre and is quite good at cooking but tends to burn cakes.

Dylan and the Deadly Dimension

By Mark Bardwell

One morning Dylan finds a snake looking up at him from the plug hole in his bathroom. That is the beginning of a series of strange events that lead him to discover a mysterious book shop with a sinister book seller and the Deadly Dimension which devours planets like a black hole.

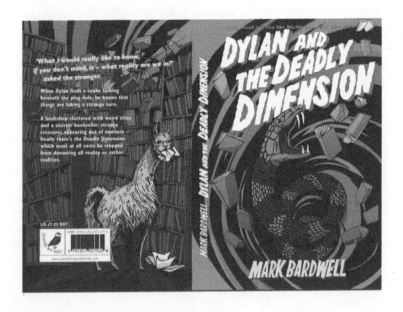

Once in a Blue Moon

By Miranda Twist

Henry's dad knows twenty-six reasons why trolls don't exist, all of them very logical, very reasonable reasons except...except that there is a troll in the wood at the bottom of their garden, the smallest troll in the world, and the wood is full of other strange creatures too: the garingay who can steal anything—even the horn of a unicorn—and the yo-yitsoo who want to punish him for for saying that trolls don't exist by turning him into a pelican with the tail of a fox. The wood is full of dangerous magic and no-one with any sense would go there but when the moon is blue, it's a wild place. The moon *is* blue and Henry's dad is deep in the wood, in a cage, turned into a pelican-fox while the yo-yitsoo and the garingay are having a party...